SLOW RIDE : BAD BOY AUTOS

DRIVE ME WILD #3

BRONWEN EVANS

SLOW RIDE
DRIVE ME WILD—Bad Boy Autos

Published By Bronwen Evans July 2021

Copy Editor: Ray Collet
Cover: Les

SLOW RIDE

From USA Today Bestselling Author, Bronwen Evans, comes her latest sexy contemporary romance! A friends-with-benefits romance with her best friend's elder brother, set in Bad Boy Autos.

Marcus Black, the ex-Formula One world champion, battles daily with the pain from the injuries he received in his career ending crash. The only way he copes is with a regular diet of booze, bills and women. Rich, charismatic, and hot as sin, to others his life looks perfect. But one woman knows better. *His Stella*. His sexy as hell, long-term friend with benefits. Only one problem... She's put an end to their arrangement just when he needs her the most.

Stella Perry has it all. A trust fund large enough to last several lifetimes and men who flock to her at the bat of her eyelashes. With parent's who have married multiple times, marriage has never been on her radar—until now. But she's made a huge mistake. She's fallen for Marcus, her friend with benefits, a man who thinks LOVE is a dirty word. Her sole option is to walk away. Only now he needs her help to beat his opiate addiction. She'll help, but then it *really* is over. Although his sexy smile and sinful body make keeping her vow to walk away virtually impossible...

I hope you enjoy the ride...

If you'd like to keep up with my other releases, my newsletter coupon codes for specials, or other news, feel free to **join my**

newsletter and receive a **FREE** book too. You can also join the newsletter on my website.

www.bronwenevans.com

PROLOGUE

Los Angeles, Cedars-Sinai hospital 3 years ago

The first thing Marcus noticed when he came out of his medically induced, drugged haze was the smell. He'd always hated the cloying stench of hospitals. He'd spent too many months during his teens, visiting his sister, Kendra, when leukemia saw her spend days and weeks in the antiseptic smelling, bleak environment of a sterile ward.

I'm still in hospital. No surprise given three weeks ago he'd broken just about every bone in his body, including his back, in a car going over 150mph.

The second thing he noticed—couldn't escape more like— was the pain. *Yep, it fuckin' hurt.* There wasn't one part of his body that didn't feel like it was being run over, again and again. His heart started racing as his throbbing head took mere moments to replay the crash in exquisite detail.

Flashes of frightening images filled his mind; metal flying apart and flames bursting from the engine with searing heat, and again, pain. His stomach clenched as he fought down the nausea.

"He's progressing better than we expected. The head injury

was not as bad as we thought, and his cognitive functions are good. His ribs and broken arm will take a few weeks to heal, as will his broken femur, but it's his back we're concerned with."

"The surgeon in Monaco told us he might be paralyzed?"

Stinky fear filled his nostrils at his father's words. He licked his lips, wishing his mouth wasn't so dry. Too scared to move his toes in case those words were true, he tried to form words, but his tongue stuck to the roof of his mouth. Suddenly beeps sounded like a shrill whistle in the room. *Yes, I'm awake,* he wanted to yell at them, *stop talking about me as if I'm not here.*

"We don't believe so. If we prick his feet, he reacts. However, he's not completely out of the woods. The disc damage to his back is significant and could create ongoing problems, if not now, perhaps later."

All Marcus heard was *not paralyzed,* and as he wiggled a toe, the beeps still piercing the air slowed to a steady blip.

"He'll need extensive physical therapy once his broken bones heal. He's extremely lucky and the surgeon in Monaco did an excellent job."

"My son is a fighter. He'll bounce back and be racing in Formula One again before you know it."

"I very much doubt that, Mr. Black. Your son's back required fusing and he won't have the strength required to sit in a small sports car for long periods without being in agonizing pain."

The beeping sound picked up once more. *His career.* His Formula One racing career he'd worked so hard for was over? Not if he had anything to say about it. He was the current world champion, and he had every intention of winning again this year.

"Besides, he has months of recuperation to get through. This season is over for him."

The doctor spelled out the end of his career as if he were discussing a day at the beach.

"Ah, you're joining us once again, Mr. Black. I was just explaining to your father you're making a splendid recovery."

"Water," his voice scratched out.

A glass with a straw met his lips. He followed the hairy arm up to see his best friend, and head mechanic, Thomas Lorde, was his water boy.

Tom smiled. "You'll do anything to gain the ladies' attention."

With his thirst momentarily quenched, he couldn't hold his head up any longer. "Care to swap places?"

Tom's smile died, and he couldn't look Marcus in the eyes.

"Any news on what caused the crash?"

"They are still reviewing the footage and cars. I'm sure we'll know soon enough," his father replied. Was that why Tom couldn't look at him?

"There was nothing wrong with the car, Tom. It was bloody Colter." Marcus closed his eyes against the pain. He hadn't even enough strength to curse out Jason Colter, his rival, and the man who'd sent his car into the wall.

"Don't worry about that now. Concentrate on getting better. I'm sick of keeping your women at bay."

He really wanted to smile at Tom's words, but the pain was building. A nurse appeared and pushed the button on the drip, and thank God for small mercies, the pain subsided, slowly. He tried to keep his eyes open but...

THE ROOM WAS QUIET WHEN HE NEXT WOKE, AND ONLY THE SOFT sound of his blipping heart monitor filled the room. He was thirsty again. Before he could raise his head off the pillow, a straw was before his mouth, but this time the arm holding the cup was slim, toned, tanned, and smooth.

"Boys and their toys. What was I always telling you?"

Stella. He smiled through the pain as he took in the fair-haired beauty holding the glass. "Speed kills, but, honey, I ain't dead." Nope, one part of him was very much alive. It twitched, even though his body ached with pain. Stella could always get his motor running.

"Kendra's getting me a proper coffee. We're here to ensure you do as the doctor orders." She paused and the 'old lady' scowl disappeared, replaced by the sexy smile he loved. "And to keep that tribe of groupies away from your door. I'm pretty sure you're in no condition to be entertaining."

"You'd be surprised." But she was right. He was in no condition.

"When you've recovered, you can surprise me plenty," she purred, making his balls swell. She was the hottest thing he'd ever seen. Guys took one look at her and sex was all they saw, but there was much more to Stella. She was intelligent, sassy, and so much fun in bed and out. Her only drawback was she was best friends with Kendra, and keeping his life private from his nosey sister was always a problem when it came to Stella.

Whenever he came home from Europe, he craved his hook ups with Stella. They'd been friends with benefits since hooking up at Kendra's twentieth birthday drinks at the Porter Club two years ago. She was the only woman he'd had any kind of consistent relationship with. A life traveling the Formula One circuit made any other type of relationship impossible.

Stella was the female version of him. Her opening line that night at the bar had been, "I do sex, really well actually, but I'm shit at relationships. I'm a screw him, thank him, then leave him kind of gal, so don't go falling in love with me."

He'd never wanted a woman more.

If his body wasn't wracked with pain, he'd take her. Hell, even with morphine flooding his body, or perhaps because of it, he wanted her.

As if sensing his thoughts, she leaned close so her breasts pressed to his chest. "Perhaps if you're a good boy, and do what the doctor orders, I'll wear my sexy nurse's uniform next time I visit."

An image flashed in his head, and blood fled south. His dick didn't seem to get the message that the rest of him was out of action. When he healed, she would be the one flat on her back.

Just then, his little sis entered the room. Kendra handed a coffee to Stella, elbowing her out of the way to bend down and hug him, whispering in his ear, "I don't want you ever racing again. I can't lose you, and Connor needs his uncle."

He looked at Stella as Kendra sobbed against his chest. She, too, had a tear in her eye.

He bit back a response. After all, it was his career that was over. If anyone should cry, it was him.

He'd make Jason Colter pay if it was the last thing he did.

CHAPTER ONE

aui, The Four Seasons Resort

For the first time since he'd gotten off the plane in Maui, Marcus's back pain was bearable and this time it wasn't because he'd popped a pill. The flight from Los Angeles to Maui, with the one stop in Honolulu, was about seven hours too long and too long for his back to be sitting in a seat, even if it was in business class. It was coming up to three years on from his accident and his back still saw him live in agony.

He rolled off the portable massage table set up in his hotel room and wrapped the towel around his waist. Part of the excitement about attending Kade and Lexie's wedding here at The Four Seasons Resort was Stella was in the bridal party too. For what he had in mind, his back needed to be, if not pain free, at least bearable.

He missed his friend with benefits. Stella had been so busy of late, apparently with some charity she had started, that they hadn't been able to hook up for quite a while. He hoped to change that this weekend. He refused to look too closely at why Stella was on his mind so much.

He walked Marianne to the door and pressed a generous tip into her hand. His money brought out a seductive smile, but he was taken for the next few days, he hoped. "I'm here all weekend if you need me," she added, as she thanked him and walked off.

"Making new friends already, I see."

He peered along the corridor. *Stella.* He couldn't help but smile. She looked amazing, dressed in an off the shoulder white linen top and jean shorts that showcased her amazing legs. Already he longed to have them wrapped around him. "Masseuse. Plane trips are a killer."

He noted her hostile stare vanished, and concern flooded her lovely blue eyes instead. "How is your back?" she asked, walking toward him, her ponytail of long blonde hair swinging in time with her hips.

"The usual. I'll cope." He stepped forward, dressed in only a towel, and heard his hotel room door click shut behind him. He spun round on a curse. "Shit. I'm locked out." *How fortuitous.* He faced Stella. "I'll wait in your room while they send up a spare key card."

She laughed. "Or I should give all the women in the hotel a treat and make you go down to reception in that skimpy towel."

"Come on, give me a break. I'm covered in oil and need a hot shower to help my back." Why not go for the pity vote?

Stella shook her head and turned back to her room a few doors down from his. "Come on, then."

"When did you arrive?" he asked as he followed her in.

She threw her hat and suntan lotion on the table. "Yesterday, with Lexie and Kendra. Lexie's so excited about her big day."

"Are the guys here?"

"Yep. They arrived this morning. The pre-wedding dinner starts at 8pm tonight. Don't be late, and I want you on your best behavior. Tomorrow, during the wedding ceremony, you'll be standing next to Jason Colter."

His fists clenched at the name. He'd hated Jason for so many years, and when Jason was an alcoholic, opiate addicted arse-hole, that was easy. Everyone felt sorry for Marcus because they blamed Jason for his crash. But now Colter had been cleared of causing his crash, and with his drug habit behind him, the bastard was sober and an upstanding citizen. If Marcus let his hatred show, *he* appeared to be the arsehole.

Life was so unfair.

He did what most men do when they don't want to answer. He changed the subject. "Can you please ring down to reception to get me a new key card while I use your shower?" Stella sighed at his lack of affirmation on the behavior front. With an encour-aging wink, he added, "Feel free to join me."

Five minutes later, he realized Stella wouldn't be joining him. *Damn.* Why had he let Jason get under his skin? If he'd simply agreed to play nice, Stella could have relieved his tension.

He grabbed one of the hotel's toweling robes in Stella's bath-room, and with his anger burning low, joined her. She was busy mixing a drink.

He came up behind her and enveloped her in his arms, pulling her back against him, letting her soft curves cool his anger. He should have left off the robe, but even through the soft toweling he could feel her heat, and the orchid scent she always wore filled his senses. His dick hardened instantly.

His lips found her neck, and he nibbled as his hands explored her body. She had tiny breasts, but they were oh, so responsive. Her nipples formed tight peaks, and he was eager to taste them. She turned in his embrace and her arms slipped around his neck on a sexy moan. She rubbed against his erec-tion. He found her mouth, and her tongue met his for a duel, which of course he won. This is what he needed. He always forgot the constant pain in his back when he held a beautiful woman in his arms.

When he held Stella in his arms.

He backed her towards the bed, but before he could tumble them onto it, she broke off the kiss and pushed out of his hold.

"Tempting as you are, big guy, I need a drink and a shower, and you need to go back to your room and get dressed. Find Jason and sort your shit out."

Another thing he could blame Jason for—cock blocking. He didn't have his watch on. "It can't be that late?"

She'd returned to making the drink. Okay, something was off.

"A beer for me, thanks," he said as he ignored her hint to leave and instead took a chair on her balcony over-looking the sea. Stella's mention of Jason was a reminder that this wedding was going to be hell, and a beer was a great way to start the weekend since a romp between the sheets appeared to be off the table.

"I suggest you have a drink with Jason before the dinner. Get out whatever it is you want to say, beat him to a pulp if you have to, but don't bring this pissed off attitude to the pre-wedding dinner or the wedding. Kendra will never forgive you. As for the bride; Lexie would kick your ass."

"Why is it I'm the bad guy here when fuckin' Jason was the one who—"

"They never found him guilty of causing the crash."

If Stella said 'let it go' he would—what? He took a long slug of his beer. What would he do? Scream like a girl? And why was it he couldn't let it go?

Her tone softened. "I know what the end of your career meant to you. I know how long it took you to recover. I was there, remember? But look at you now. You love Bad Boy Autos. It's a tremendous success, and you don't need the title of world champion race car driver to attract the women. They drop into your bed on a smile."

"No, they don't," he muttered under his breath.

"Don't be modest."

"You didn't join me in the shower." He waited for the usual snappy, edgy reply, but it never came. He looked at her. His gut clenched as he watched her down her drink in one long swallow. "Why *didn't* you join me in the shower? Why aren't we in your bed right now? Neither of us brought a date to this wedding."

"I need another drink." She made her way inside, and he heard the ice cubes clank. Something was up with his Stella. *His Stella?* When had she become his Stella? He rose and followed her inside.

"Have you met someone?" Her back stiffened at his words, and for one moment he feared the worse.

"No."

He let out the breath he'd been holding. "Then what's up?" She wasn't the same. Normally she'd have him out of this robe, naked on the bed and straddled before he'd dried himself off from the shower. Hell, she would have been with him in the shower, down on her knees...

She turned to face him. *Shit.* He knew instantly he wouldn't like what she had to say.

"I think it's time we called an end to our friends with benefits arrangement."

Yep. Something was definitely up, and it wasn't his dick. "Why?" What he should have asked himself was why the idea of Stella not being his friend with amazing benefits made him feel like his world was ending, but he wasn't drunk enough to face himself.

"The view is beautiful on the balcony." She took his hand and led him back outside. "Besides, you need to be sitting down for this. You wouldn't believe me if I told you."

"Try me," he insisted.

Shielding her eyes from the setting sun, she sighed. "I blame your sister."

"What's Kendra got to do with this?"

"She's happy. She and Tom... their children, Connor and Matti. They are so happy together." She turned to him, with tears welling in her eyes. "I don't know if I've ever been as content as they are, but I know I want to experience what they have. I want that someone special. Marriage and children even."

He swallowed slowly. "Are you telling me you want the white picket fence and happy families? I thought we both agreed there was no such thing?"

"Maybe we're wrong. Maybe if you find the right person..."

If she wasn't looking so teary and serious, he would have laughed. Right person! Yeah, right? There was no such thing. Her movie producer father was onto wife number five or was it six, and his father... His parents didn't share the same bedroom, let alone the same bed and hadn't for years. God knows how he and Kendra were ever conceived.

Marcus wasn't giving up yet. "So what? Let's keep our arrangement on the table until the right man comes along, or at least for the wedding." Stella would come around. She just needed a reminder of how great they were in bed.

She shook her head. "I'm serious, Marcus. No more FWB. I'm not likely to find a potential husband with the hunky guy who I have sex with hanging around."

"Well, that's made this wedding even more unbearable."

Stella laughed. "Oh, please. You'll find a replacement for me before the dinner tonight, I bet."

He didn't want a replacement. He wanted Stella.

"Don't look at me like that," she said softly.

"Like what?"

"Like I'm the only woman in the world for you. That's not fair, because for you it's not true. You aren't a one-woman kind of guy, and you're not interested in marriage."

She was bloody right there, but losing... it wasn't just about losing the sex, fuckin' fantastic as it was between them, it was the idea of losing this. The one person he could be himself with.

The woman who didn't give a shit about his celebrity status or how much money he had. The one person he could really talk to. His body grew cold even with the heavy bath robe on.

He was losing Stella, and he didn't know what to do about it, or why it mattered so much.

He drew in a deep breath and really looked at her. She was staring at the sunset, sadness hanging over her. He didn't want her sad. He reached out and took her delicate hand in his. They sat in silence, watching the sun go down. It was going down on their relationship and friendship. Whatever he had with Stella would never be the same, and it tore him up inside.

In the dimming light, he stood and leaned down to kiss her cheek. "I hope you find Mr. Right, if he exists. I want you to be happy. Life's too short. I'm always here if you need me." She rolled her eyes. "I'm not talking about sex, you wicked girl, but it's always on the table. I'll remind you in case you have forgotten, but the F in FWB stands for friends."

She didn't reply. What could she say that she hadn't already said? It was over, and he hated how it made him feel. *Scared.* He'd always had Stella on his side since before the accident. She'd been there when he wondered if he'd ever walk again. Now he had no one.

He took his leave, picking his new key card off the table, and called over his shoulder, "I'm off to find Jason. Will Lexie kill me if he has a black eye in the wedding photos?"

"No, but Kade, his brother-you know, the groom-might."

The door to her hotel room closed behind him on her laughter, but Marcus couldn't laugh. It was sinking in that he'd probably lost the best thing in his life and it sucked.

CHAPTER TWO

I *did it. I told him.* She knew ending her relationship with Marcus would hurt, but she hadn't expected to see the matching hurt in his eyes. That'd really ripped her heart out. Was there more to their arrangement than she thought? Could Marcus have deeper feelings for her? Had she done the right thing?

She sipped her rum and coke and let the tears fall. She'd told him, but she'd told him only the half of it. She was in love with him. She wanted him to be her special someone, but after nine months of slowly drawing away, nine months of making herself unavailable, he'd not bothered to chase after her. It would appear any woman would do.

She swiped the tears from her face with the back of her hand. She wanted to be Marcus's only woman. She wanted a genuine relationship, something Marcus didn't know how to do. Tears were useless.

Why did he have to look so damn hot? God, wandering around her room in a skimpy towel, with all those wash-board abs on display... she deserved a flipping medal for not jumping his bones.

She loved running her tongue over each ripple of muscle as she rode him. He was solid muscle, working on his core strength like crazy to help stabilize his damaged back. He was sex on two legs, but to her he was more than sex. That's why she had to end it. He'd be in her bed satisfying her now if sex was all she cared about.

She looked down from her top floor room and watched couples walking hand in hand through the garden below. How many of them would be together one year from now? Twenty years from now? She understood where Marcus was coming from. Her father was the walking advertisement for staying single. The only person happy about dear old Dad's serial divorcing was his lawyer.

As for her mum... all she looked for in a man was a deep wallet. Husband number three appeared to have lasted longer than most. She hoped her mother stayed with him and found some peace, having taken years to get over her father's betrayal. Good old mum fell apart and got hooked on drugs. That had left Stella to mop up the vomit and ring for the ambulance when mother dearest finally overdosed. She'd also driven her mum to rehab and thankfully it had worked.

Stella refused to ever let a guy reduce her to such hopelessness. She would never be like her mum. That was why she usually kept guys at arm's length. She didn't trust any of them.

She didn't trust Marcus. He would never lie, but he'd never agree to a relationship that he couldn't walk away from. Marcus would never marry. He thought he was too much like his dad, and he was right.

Why had she fallen in love with him, of all people?

The worst part about all of this was she had no one to confide in. Kendra was her best friend, like the sister she didn't have, but how could she talk about Marcus with Kendra? Kendra would likely hate her for getting involved with him and she'd be furious that Stella had lost her heart to her brother, because Kendra knew Marcus was a never get tied down kind of guy.

Stella yawned. It was going to be a long weekend. She rose, taking one last look at the couples down below. It was time to shower and put on her happy bridesmaid face. If Lexie could be brave and marry the brother of her ex-husband, and if Kade was happy for Jason to be in the bridal party, then Stella could face this wedding without giving in and sleeping with Marcus.

She wished he wasn't so tall, dark and handsome, or that she loved him so much. The memory of him in her bed, and how they scorched the sheets, haunted her dreams.

Worse, if he, or more like *when* he picked up a woman this weekend, Stella would have to watch and bear it, as if she was happy they were no longer bed buddies. She wasn't that strong.

Maybe she'd find the man of her dreams among the guests. She doubted it, because she pretty much knew all of Kade and Lexie's friends, and besides, who could ever win against Marcus?

Getting through the wedding would be hell.

Getting on with her life without Marcus…was there a place worse than hell?

A pounding on her door, interrupted her thoughts.

Please don't let it be Marcus, because if one foot stepped back into this room, she didn't know if she had the strength to resist him.

Her prayer was answered.

Lexie piled in the door before Stella stepped back.

The bride was all fidgety with excitement. "You're not dressed yet? What have you been doing?" Lexie spied the empty beer bottle. "Let me guess, Marcus has been here." She looked at the bed, which of course was not rumpled. "Or maybe not."

Lexie was the only one who knew about her relationship with Marcus. She'd caught them kissing late one night at Bad Boy Autos. Lexie worked as a mechanic and designer for

Marcus's upmarket chop shop, specializing in up-specking European cars like Maserati and Porsche.

"If you must know I had a drink with Marcus and ended our…arrangement."

"Before my wedding? Why did you…? No, I won't ask. It's about time, if you ask me. You deserve more."

"I do." That's why she'd ended it.

"I'll wait while you get dressed."

"I haven't even showered yet." She gently pushed Lexie toward the door. "I'll meet you downstairs, as soon as I'm presentable."

Lexie stopped. "One favor. It should be an easy one now you've broken it off with Marcus."

She crossed her arms. "I'm not saying yes until I know what it is."

"It's Jason." Stella's mouth dropped open, but Lexie pleaded. "I know you've never really met him, but he's here on his own. As he's in the bridal party he's come solo too. I don't want him to feel like everyone is looking at him, or is against him. Could you attempt to introduce yourself and keep him company?"

Shit. Why was Lexie so worried about her ex-husband who'd put her through hell? He'd been a booze and coke addicted man-whore, and just because he'd got himself cleaned up, all should be forgiven? Lexie had nothing to be guilty about. Jason had cheated on her, abused her, and run off with her money. Kade had helped her, supported her, and given Lexie faith enough to love and trust again.

Besides, it wasn't a good idea, given she'd just broken up with Marcus, and Jason was at the top of Marcus's hate list. Marcus, to this day, swore it was Jason's erratic driving that caused him to crash in the Monaco race. The crash that destroyed his racing career and almost left him a cripple.

She was about to say no, but Lexie chewed her lip and looked desperate. Stella hoped she didn't live to regret this. "I will not be his official watcher, but I'll ensure I talk with him, and if I see him looking lost, I'll meander to his side."

Lexie hugged her. "Thank you."

"Why are you so worried about a man who treated you like dirt?"

Lexie hugged her harder. "He was a different person then. Drugs make people do things they wouldn't normally do. Addiction is an illness."

Stella always thought addiction was for people too weak to say no; people like her mum.

Then the image of a naked Marcus going down on her flooded her head. Suddenly, she knew how hard it was to battle an addiction. Her addiction was an ex-Formula One racing car driver with come to bed eyes. If it had been Marcus, not Lexie, at her door, what would she have done?

"If you say so. Now scram, I'm running really late."

CHAPTER THREE

The next day, just after lunch, Marcus wished he'd had time to ring for Marianne, the masseuse, before the wedding. He'd only just made it through his shower.

He bent backwards, trying to stretch out his back but, after the golf he'd played today with the guys, he was fucked. He knew he shouldn't have played the last five holes, but then he'd have had to explain how bad his back had gotten and he wasn't about to let Jason win the match.

He'd gone to confront Jason last night, but the bastard beat him to it by approaching him with a groveling apology. Part of Jason's 12-step program, apparently. He'd listened, but couldn't quite accept Jason's apology. Jason hadn't mentioned the crash or apologized for it. He didn't trust Jason as far as he could kick him and he still didn't like him.

He finished his glass of scotch and made his way to the bathroom to find his toiletry bag. He hated having to rely on his pain meds, but he'd never get through this wedding without them. He'd barely made it through dinner last night and golf today had finished him off.

Stella. Stella dumped his ass. That's why he'd needed alcohol.

He shouldn't have had that scotch, but one drink shouldn't cause any major problems when mixed with his prescribed OxyContin. He needed both to block the pain, but he wouldn't drink anything else tonight. He wasn't stupid.

He downed two pills and slipped on his jacket just as someone rapped on his door.

"Bro' come on, I'm sure you're pretty enough."

He opened the door to Tom. "Fuck off."

"What's crawled up your ass?"

He could hardly say he was pissed that Stella had dumped him. Tom didn't know about their arrangement. "I have to go to a wedding and I have to stand next to Jason 'asshole' Colter."

"I get where you're coming from. I want to like the guy as he's trying to turn it around, but shit, your crash…"

Marcus hit the down button on the elevator. "You're supposed to be getting me out of my foul mood. Let's not mention Jason again tonight." As he stepped into the lift, he said, "How's Kade holding up?"

"Holding up? Christ man, he's not going to his execution. He's getting married to the woman he loves. He's beside himself with excitement."

Marcus shrugged. "I'll ask him how happy he is in two year's time."

Tom stood, shaking his head. "Man. I thought you'd mellow as you got older. You know, grow the fuck up. There is more to life than getting laid by a different woman every night."

"Not for me."

"I used to be like you until I manned up and realized what I have with Kendra is what makes life worth living. What are you living for?"

His body jerked as Tom's question sank in or was it the elevator coming to a juddery stop? What did he live for? His throat clogged with emotion as he stepped out of the elevator.

Tom walked past him and clapped him on the back. "Think about it, bro."

Kade met them as they walked out into the sunshine. The ceremony would be held on the beach at 5pm, with dinner in a private area of the hotel's terrace. Already there were many familiar faces sitting in the small gathering as he made his way down the aisle to stand with the other groomsmen. Jason was already there and Marcus ignored the smile the man sent in his direction.

As he stood waiting for the wedding to start, Marcus looked out over the beautiful sea. Kade and Lexie had picked a lovely place to tie the knot. The beach was fairly empty of people this late in the afternoon, or was it early evening, but an old couple sat on one of the benches along the path looking at the sea, holding hands, watching the sunset. They sat in silence, watching the world around them. If anything in particular caught their attention, they merely turned to each other and smiled. They didn't need words to know what the other thought. For a fleeting moment, Marcus envied them. That bond of two people who have shared a life together and who have unconditional love and respect for each other was a pipe dream for most.

The warmth of this setting was rudely smashed out of focus by an image of his parents sitting in their living room when he was a teenager; his father with the paper held up in front of him, as if he couldn't bear to look at his wife, his mother knitting with a glass of wine within reach. The quietness wasn't welcoming. His skin crawled every time he'd had to sit in the same room with them, and suffer the hostile, knifing silence.

How did some people get marriage so right while others didn't? Bitterness sank into his heart as he watched the older man stand and help his wife up. Maybe if his parent's marriage had been different…. They linked arms and began a slow stroll along the waterfront. For a fleeting moment, he wished—no.

He'd be a terrible husband. He was too much like his father. Driven, competitive, selfish, arrogant. He was not marriage material. He wouldn't ruin a woman's life like his father had, destroying his fun-loving mother until she was a drunken mouse.

Music started and his bad mood lifted as he turned and spied Stella leading the procession. She looked stunning and sexy in her light blue floaty dress. The spaghetti straps showed off her arms and breasts. Her fair hair was piled high on her head, and he longed to run his lips down her slender neck. His gut tightened as he realized he'd never have that joy again.

She was beautiful and he couldn't take his eyes off her, even when Lexie took center stage and walked down the aisle.

A flush covered Stella's face as she realized he was staring at her throughout the wedding ceremony. She fidgeted with her hair and dress, as if looking for something wrong.

Thank goodness it wasn't long before they were side by side at a small table.

She whispered, "I haven't got my dress tucked in my g-string, have I?"

"No." His mind flashed to an image of a thong. She never wore anything else. He loved peeling them off her with his teeth.

"Then why were you staring?"

He shrugged. "You look beautiful."

She held his gaze, then looked away. "That's not fair. You can't say things like that to me anymore."

"Why not?"

"Because we are no longer having that kind of relationship. Would you say that to Lexie?" He wouldn't and Stella put the boot in further. "And no more staring or sending seductive smiles my way. You're wasting those come to bed eyes on me."

Before he could answer, she walked forward to hold Lexie's bouquet while she signed the marriage register.

He needed to lift his game if he wanted to persuade Stella to reinstate their FWB arrangement.

"You've crashed into the wall there, Marcus, and I had nothing to do with it."

He swung round on Jason, about to follow through with his fist, when he remembered his promise to Stella. He stepped back and adjusted his tie. "Stella is just a friend."

"Really? Another thing you're lying to yourself about," said Jason, as he moved on with that 'you're full of shit' smile on his face.

"He's got you there," Tom uttered, as he came to stand beside him to watch Jason sign the marriage document of his ex-wife to his own brother. "It's unlike you to try to hit on Kendra's friends. They know your rep too well," Tom laughed.

"I wasn't hitting on her." *I was trying to win her back.*

"Good. Kendra would kill you if you messed with Stella."

Why did that scare him more than the sharks that could be lurking in the bay he'd swum in this morning?

"Stella can look after herself. She has broken a few hearts." Marcus wondered why she'd never met Mr. Right. She'd had enough chances. It was as he'd told her. There's no such thing as Mr. Right, only Mr. Right for now.

Tom dug him in the ribs with his elbow. "The happy couple look more than happy if there is such a thing. I remember the feeling well. Every time Kendra and I have a hic up, I remember how happy we were on our wedding day and I stop sweating the little shit. It's like they say, 'happy wife, happy life'."

"Besides, Kendra's usually right."

"You have to say that she's your sister."

The men watched as Kendra walked towards them, having signed the register. "When am I going to get to come to your wedding?" She asked, as she hooked her arm through his.

"When hell freezes over and since we have global warming, that's not likely to happen."

Instead of her normal smart reply, Kendra leaned back and looked at him for a moment. "What's sad is you believe that, but I think you're lonely. Maybe I'll make it my mission to find you someone to spend your life with."

He laughed. "I don't have trouble finding women, sister dear. I have trouble wanting them to hang around longer than breakfast the next morning."

"I'm surprised you even give them breakfast," Tom mumbled.

"Come on, you two. I hope I won't get this shit all weekend. This is why I hate attending weddings."

Stella arrived, with Jason by her side, and Marcus's hackles rose. Was she flirting with Jason on purpose?

"I need a drink." He turned and made his way to the bar, set up on the terrace, overlooking the sand and turquoise blue ocean. He sensed Tom following. "Coke, please."

"Coke for me too, and 3 glasses of champagne for the ladies." Tom leaned against the bar as they waited for their drinks. "Coke for you? What's up with that?"

"Just need to slow down after last night. I told Kendra I'd be on my best behavior and having Colter here... I need a clear head." He hated lying, but with the pills he was popping, drinking was not a good idea.

It pleased him he'd stuck to Coke when they made their way to dinner and he sat next to Stella and discovered bloody Colter was on her other side. Marcus flashed dagger eyes at Lexie, but the bride simply smiled sweetly. She'd done this on purpose. She was the only one who knew about him and Stella. What game was she playing?

Fuck it. When the server offered him a glass of champers, he took it. It wasn't really his drink, but hell, Jason's smile as he sat next to Stella was the last straw. If Jason thought he had a chance with Stella, he was more delusional than anyone thought. Perhaps Jason was back snorting coke up his nose. He could only hope.

As the meal progressed, Marcus tried to ignore the conversation going on to his left between Stella and Jason. When he dropped his fork onto his plate, splattering food, Stella put her hand on his knee under the table, squeezed it and whispered, "How much have you had to drink?"

"Just this glass of champagne."

She looked at him skeptically. "Well, you must have had a few before the wedding."

Pissed now. "I had one scotch. Anyway, what's it to you? You're not my mother."

The hand disappeared, and he cursed under his breath. He really hated weddings, and this one was about as bearable as having a tooth pulled, without anesthetic.

Thank God the meal and speeches were over quickly. He had to admit that when Kade escorted Lexie onto the dance floor for their first dance the love between the two was visible. They only had eyes for each other, and he wondered if he could ever love one woman the way Kade loved Lexie. Is this why he never tried? He loathed failure. Win at all costs was his motto. He would never have become a world champion without the killer instinct to win.

Stella whispered. "They look so happy. Do you still think there isn't that perfect person for each of us out there?"

He had to admit that they looked perfect together. He could imagine them as the old couple on the bench by the sea, but before he could answer, Jason arrived.

"When you find the one, it's important not to fuck it up. I should know."

Stella smiled at Jason, and Marcus's gut clenched. "I think it's wonderful how you are happy for them. Attending your ex-wife's wedding to your brother can't be easy."

"She deserves to find happiness. I wasn't good to Lexie. She was so sad all the time, and Kade made her smile again. If only we could turn back time as Cher says." Jason moved close to Stella and said, "When I meet a woman who is special, I won't make that mistake again. Care for a dance, gorgeous?"

Marcus didn't know how he stood there and let Jason lead her onto the dance floor. Instead, he turned and walked to the bar, but he couldn't have alcohol. He'd already had two glasses and with the pills....he sighed. "Another Coke, please."

CHAPTER FOUR

S tella decided if she ever married she wanted a wedding just like this; small, intimate and at the most stunning beach front resort setting. She had no actual family, no brothers or sisters, only her parents, so a big church would look bare. She had her venue, now all she needed was the man!

She was taking a breather out on the beach, sitting in the sand, when Kendra ran across, looking like she was crying. "My brother, sometimes I could kill him."

"What's he done now?"

"He's drunk. He mouthed off to Jason and then it was all on."

Stella jumped to her feet. Shit. This was her fault. She just couldn't resist flirting with Jason. She'd wanted a reaction, and she supposed this was it. "The barman shouldn't have served him drinks if he was that drunk."

She took off toward the bar, wanting someone to take her guilt out on. When she got there, she beckoned the young man over. "Why did you keep serving my friend when he'd obviously had too much to drink? I have a notion to talk to your manager."

He frowned. "He's only been ordering Coke. I haven't served him anything with alcohol in it."

Stella's mouth fell open. Her brain went into overdrive. Something was wrong. "Sorry, my mistake."

She looked round the room and spotted Kade. She made her way through the other guests and asked, "Where has Marcus gone?"

"Tom took him to his room to sleep it off. I have to say he won't be flavor of the month tomorrow. Lexie's pretty upset at them both. Jason should have known better than to egg Marcus on when he was obviously out of it."

At her frown, Kade raised an eyebrow. "What? He's drunk. He was weaving all over the place."

"The barman swears Marcus has been drinking Coke all night."

Kade ran a hand through his hair. "Shit. Then this is bloody Jason's fault. Sometimes I could almost hate my brother. He's ruined it for Lexie, once again."

"I can kind of understand Jason's rationale. He's had to face what he's lost. That can't be easy."

"Jason's in AA and turning his life around. He has no excuse to fight." Kade looked at her again. "Are you sure Marcus wasn't drinking? The only reason Jason got such a good punch in was Marcus appeared to be unsteady on his feet."

Stella bit her bottom lip. "There's only one way to find out. I'll check on him." Marcus had given her a key card since he had a spare. No doubt hopeful she'd turn up in his room. Well, he'd got his wish.

WHEN STELLA ENTERED MARCUS'S HOTEL ROOM, THE ONLY LIGHT illuminating the room was from the moon shining through the windows. Thankfully, with the curtains open, it took mere moments to find Marcus in the gloom, slumped on one of the chairs in the room's corner, head resting in his hands. Could a man look any more miserable?

He's brought this on himself, she reminded herself. *Be strong, don't feel sorry for him.*

Anger tried to rise its formidable head, but he looked so pitiful it dissipated like a mist after sunrise. As she moved towards him, he lifted his head.

"I know you're angry. I know everyone's angry, but I swear I haven't been drinking."

She took his hands in hers, as she crouched at his feet. "Well, you're certainly not sober. Kade could see that by the end of the night you were swaying all over the place, but I spoke to the barman and he swears you were drinking Coke most of the night. What's going on?"

"Nothing. I swear."

Why couldn't he look her in the eye? He was lying. "Then the only conclusion I can draw is you purposely picked a fight with Jason to ruin Lexi's wedding. Is that what you want me to think?"

"Bloody, Colter. I know I should have stayed away but…"

"Why did you come to the wedding? You're not really a wedding kind of guy."

He looked at her, and his hand reached out to cup her chin. "Because you would be here and you've been avoiding me. I wanted to see you."

That confirmed it. He had to be drunk or… shit, high. No way would he admit this vulnerability when sober.

She couldn't reply. She didn't want to read anything into his words because of what would happen when he sobered up. "Let me see your face."

She switched on the table lamp beside them. Blood had dried under his nose and he had a slight cut above his eyebrow. "Let's get you cleaned up."

He didn't move as she made her way to the bathroom, finding a flannel, and running it under warm water. She filled a glass with water. He'd have a pounding head in the morning and she wondered if he had any Tylenol. His toiletry bag lay open by the sink. She searched through and her hand hit a prescription bottle. When Stella read the label, her hand shook. Things made sense. Tom had told her as they passed in the corridor that Marcus had only had one glass of champagne at the wedding. But on top of OxyContin—and she didn't know how many—she was pretty sure Marcus was as high as a skyscraper.

She stood looking at herself in the mirror, the water still running, while memories of her mother's addiction to pain meds filled her head with images she'd rather forget.

How long had he been taking these? His back must be bad or... had he simply become addicted to the pain meds? She looked at the label again. It was from his doctor. Surely if he had a problem, Dr. Forrester wouldn't be supplying him?

She tucked the pills back into his toiletry bag. She needed to talk with him, but she'd wait until tomorrow morning when he was sober.

She hesitated before going back into the bedroom. What if Marcus *was* addicted to pain meds? *Not your problem.*

She didn't owe him anything. They'd had sex, that was all. He didn't want any commitment. She would inform Kendra and let her look after her brother.

As she walked towards him, misery cloaking him, her heart clenched in her chest. To the world it might look like Marcus Black had everything; money, fame, good looks, but having been a friend of the family all her life, and Kendra's best friend, Stella knew that it had come at a cost. From an early age, Marcus's father had pushed him to win. The Blacks never lost which was why Mr. Black refused to grant his wife a divorce, why he disowned Kendra when she got pregnant and refused to name the father, and why Marcus was so lost when his career ended.

What was she going to do with him?

After cleaning his face and getting him to drink plenty of water, she stood up.

"Let's get you into bed."

"Yes, please," he whispered, as he stood and leaned in to kiss her.

"Alone. To sleep this off."

"You're no fun, anymore."

"That's because I want more than just fun, and that scares you."

Like a little boy, he let her lead him to the bed. She helped him take off his clothes, down to his boxers.

He closed his eyes as his head hit the pillow. Her heart couldn't help hurting. It would be so easy to spoon in behind him, to cuddle him through the night, but in the morning nothing would have changed. He won't have changed.

She closed the door quietly as she left Marcus's room. Tomorrow she would talk with him and find out how bad the pain in his back had become.

If he wouldn't tell her, she'd work on a way to make him tell her.

An idea formed.

CHAPTER FIVE

The next morning, Stella organized food to be sent to Marcus before she slipped out of her room and made her way along the corridor to his, and let herself in. He was fast asleep, on his back, arms flung wide, with the sheet hanging low on his hips. He looked good enough to eat and she wanted him more than the pancakes she'd just ordered.

At ten in the morning the sun shone, the day was getting hotter and she wanted answers. She plonked her bum down on the side of the bed, none too gently. One of Marcus's eyes opened and he groaned.

"Leave me alone. It can't be morning yet."

"It's gone ten o'clock and I'll not let you waste the day sleeping. We have to meet Kade and Lexi for lunch before they jet off to New Zealand for their honeymoon."

Marcus's reply was to groan again, roll away from her and pull the sheet over his head. Thank God, as looking at his naked, muscled torso was raising her temperature. Before she could disgrace herself by joining him between the sheets, there was a knock on the door.

She jumped up. "That'll be room service. I ordered breakfast. While I set it up on the balcony, please get in the shower." She ripped the sheet from him, knowing he'd had his boxers on last night. More's the pity, she thought, as she skipped to answer the door.

Thankfully, she heard him rise and enter the bathroom with no further cajoling. She signed for the food and left a large tip. Marcus could afford it. He'd made a fortune on the racing circuit in prize money and endorsements, but it was his vision for Bad Boy Autos that saw his wealth multiply.

After his accident near on three years ago, Marcus and Tom, who'd been his head mechanic on the Formula One racing circuit, set up a high-end car modification business. Wealthy men, who wanted faster, more agile, one-of-a-kind cars, brought their Porsche, Lamborghini and Aston Martin vehicles to Bad Boy Autos to be customized. Who wouldn't want an ex-formula one champion test driving your one-off customized car?

She took breakfast out to the balcony, overlooking the ocean, and set it up on the table. So domesticated. She sighed. Why was she putting herself through this? She longed for this to be real, to have Marcus as her partner, enjoying a holiday together before going home to their house with the white picket fence.

It had taken her years to understand that the marriages she'd experienced in her life—her father had married five times, and her mother three—were not the norm for others. Love was not disposable if you found the right person. The couple who gave meaning to her life by showing her how she could use her good fortune to help others, Sofia and Charles, let her see into a different world than the one she'd grown up in.

They'd been married for thirty-five years, had four beautiful children together, and when Charles looked at Sofia it was always with a look of complete devotion, that brought tears to Stella's eyes.

She poured a cup of coffee and sat on the lounger, hugging her dream to herself. The view lifted her spirits, but she chided herself for her foolish dream. Marcus would never change, or maybe it was simply that he didn't view a relationship with her as worth changing for. Then why was she here this morning?

She was the only one who had an inkling something was wrong with him, and she knew this because she was probably the only person Marcus had let get inside his barriers. As far as she knew, their FWB was the longest and only relationship he'd had with anyone other than his sister, and Kendra seemed to have no idea how bad Marcus's back issues had become. What concerned her more was, neither did Tom.

Finally, Marcus appeared, freshly showered, with his black hair still wet and slicked back, and dressed in shorts and his signature light pink Polo shirt. With his sunglasses on he looked like he'd just stepped out of a fashion photo shoot. *Be still my beating heart. Be still my hormones more like.*

She poured him a coffee and pushed a plate full of pancakes, bacon and strawberries at him.

"How mad is Lexie?"

"Do you really want to know?"

"Shit. So, a bunch of flowers won't cut it?"

"Not unless it was a standing order every day for the rest of your life." And even then, Stella wasn't sure that would be enough. "A girl only gets married once."

"Really? Isn't this Lexie's second wedding? And to another Colter?"

Blast. Wrong thing to say to Marcus. "I intend to only get married once."

"Unlike your father, because you're going to marry Mr. Right," he laughed. His laugh faded. "I'm really sorry about last night. I don't know what came over me."

"Too many OxyContin perhaps?"

He looked up like a startled rabbit. "How did—"

"I was looking for something for your sore head last night. How long have you been taking them?"

"My doctor prescribes them."

"I know that or else I'd have Tom and Kendra here, too. How long?"

Marcus sighed and pushed his plate away from him. "Just over eight months."

"And the doctor is okay with that?"

He ran a hand through his hair. She wished he'd take the sunglasses off, as she couldn't see his eyes. "Not particularly, but we're working through some options."

That made her sit up. "Options? For what?"

He sat in silence for a moment. "My back's getting worse. They're recommending surgery."

"Why are you hesitant?"

He swung round to face her. "It's surgery. I'd be on my back for months, and there is no guarantee it will work."

She reined in her temper. "But you can't live on these pills for much longer. You understand how addictive they are and what they could do to your kidneys, and liver. I can't believe your doctor is still prescribing them. My mother—"

"I like that you're worried for me, but I'm not your mother. I'm made of sterner stuff." Marcus reached for her hand. "I have it under control. Forrester's prescribing less and less, trying to wean me off them, but I need them to function. Yesterday, a round of golf nearly killed me."

Her mouth dropped open and flapped like a fish, before she blurted out, "Then why the hell did you play? If it causes you pain then stop."

He growled low in his throat. "I'm in pain all the time. Would you have me just lie in bed all day, because that's what it will take for me to be pain free."

"How has your doctor let it get this bad? Why aren't you rushing to have the surgery?"

Marcus needed a drink. "I realize you mean well, Stella, but this is my problem and my life. I appreciate your concern though."

He was right. She was overstepping the bounds of...what? Friendship? Hadn't she told him she wanted to end their relationship?

"I'll leave it."

"And you're not to say anything to Tom or Kendra."

She looked at him and noted the tightness around his mouth. "I know you think you can live your life alone, letting no one in. Isn't that why you picked motor racing? You drive around a track and whether you win or lose is down to you."

He laughed. "You think Formula One racing is a solo sport? You're wrong. I had a team around me I relied on and who relied on me. If Tom and I couldn't communicate about the car, it wouldn't perform at its best. You have to be a team player to succeed. I had to earn the respect of our team or the well-oiled machine would have fallen over."

She'd never really understood the appeal of motor racing or why anyone would want to risk their life to speed around a track. "I know nothing about racing." She looked up at Marcus as he leaned back in his chair. "Look, I just hope that if things get worse, you'll tell Tom. We're all here for you."

She didn't need to see his eyes to catch the scathing look he threw her. "I don't need anyone's pity."

She rose, throwing her napkin on the table. "For goodness' sake grow up." She stood looking at him. "When are you flying home?"

"I have an open ticket. I was hoping you and I might have stayed for a few extra days. I booked us on a Molokini and Turtle Town snorkel cruise tomorrow morning. I should cancel it. I hadn't foreseen you calling off our arrangement."

She couldn't believe she was about to say this, but she wanted to see just how bad his back was before agreeing not to inform Tom or Kendra. Her mother thought she didn't need help at the beginning too, and she'd almost died. The guilt would eat her alive if Marcus ended up dead or worse from taking these legitimately prescription drugs. She needed him to open up to her and tell her what was really going on.

"Don't cancel it. I could do with a few days of relaxation. This charity event I'm organizing is exhausting. Let's stay a few more days and do the cruise tomorrow."

"Really?" Marcus sat upright in his chair. "That would be fun."

She smiled. "But as friends only, no benefits. Agreed?"

"Spoil sport." He sighed and ran a hand through his hair. "Swimming is the only time my back doesn't hurt so much. The water supports it. Besides, it's probably too late to cancel the cruise, anyway. I guess you have yourself a deal."

She bent and pressed a kiss to his forehead. "Now all you have to do is apologize to Lexie and Kade before we meet for lunch." A curse slipped from between his lips. "While you're doing that, I'll organize another back massage for you, and I'll even join you. A relaxing afternoon at the spa will do us both good."

He stood up and stretched. "Tom and Kendra are going to the airport with Lexie and Kade. The doting parents want to rush home. That will leave you and I," he said, and wiggled his eyebrows.

He was temptation all right and about as addictive as his OxyContin. "Don't look at me like that."

"Like what?" He asked, as innocent as the devil.

"No benefits. You were the one who said we could still be friends. Did you mean that or was it a line?" *Be firm.*

"I'll be good. I swear we won't do anything you don't want to do."

Shit. This was going to be an interesting few days. Both of them fighting their demons of addiction. Him, his pills and her, his lips and more…

"Fine. I'll see you at lunch?"

～

MARCUS HEARD THE DOOR CLOSE BEHIND STELLA. WHY DIDN'T HE just tell her the truth? The reason he wouldn't contemplate the surgery is because the surgeons told him he could end up paralyzed, in a wheelchair or a cripple on sticks. And he couldn't even think about the other risk…

He looked out over what should be paradise and all he felt was cold, putrid fear.

Stella was clever to call off their relationship now. He definitely couldn't be any woman's Mr. Right from a wheelchair.

He drank the rest of his coffee and tried to block the voice screaming loudly in his head 'take a pill, or two.' He reminded himself that Dr. Forrester said only one to four per day. If he kept taking them the way he had since he'd arrived on Maui, he'd run out before he got back to LA.

He stuffed his wallet in his back pocket, grabbed his key card and headed out, his pills left behind. No pills today. *He wasn't addicted.*

He was so pissed at himself for causing a scene at the wedding, and he owed Lexie. He didn't know what to buy for her. She wasn't a jewelry kind of girl. As her boss, he knew one thing he could do. He'd give her a couple of extra weeks off work to make up for his mistake. They could have a longer honeymoon.

Stepping out of the elevator in the lobby, he bumped into the one person he hoped had left already.

"Colter."

"Black. Listen, I'm sorry about last night. I should have known better than to hit a guy who was high." Jason shook his head when all Marcus did was shut his mouth. "You're not denying it? That's a good sign. If you ever want to talk..."

Marcus made to brush past him. "You'd be the last person I'd speak to."

Jason grabbed his arm. "Don't be an idiot. I'm the only one of them who would understand. I know you think I caused your crash but I didn't. I might have been close but I swear I never clipped you."

He pulled his arm free. "Too high to notice."

"I never drove under the influence of anything." Jason was probably so high he'd not known what he'd done. His team stood him down shortly after the crash.

"I didn't clip myself."

Jason ran a hand through his hair. "There were three other cars around you. It wasn't me." Marcus scoffed. "Go to hell then. When you're ready to seek help for your addiction, let me know."

Marcus walked away before he said something to start the fight back up. Addiction! He might have drunk too much last night with his pills, but he wasn't addicted. He only took them when he needed pain relief and they were doctor prescribed. Jason had bought his narcotics from drug dealers. Completely different.

As he walked into the restaurant, Stella rose from her chair and beckoned him over. The looks Kade and Lexie threw him could freeze hell.

"I don't know where to start with an apology for being such a twat last night. There is no excuse, so I'm simply going to say, sorry. Have two more weeks leave on me."

Kade broke into a big smile while Lexie looked at Stella, still looking pissed.

"I really want to stay angry at you, but Stella told us about the mix-up in your medication, I shall not hold it against you, even though you almost destroyed my special day." Then she broke into a big smile. "And the extra two weeks holiday is a thoughtful peace offering. Come, sit and let's eat."

"Tom and Kendra not joining us?" he asked, as he sat next to Stella.

"They left already and got an earlier flight." Kade replied. "It's your sister's first time away from Matti. Two nights was enough."

Shit. Kendra must be furious with him, because she didn't even let him know she was leaving early.

"Matti is a cutie. Twenty months and she is walking and just saying the odd word."

It finally hit him that Stella meant what she said about wanting a family. The longing in her voice when she talked about Matti, her God-daughter, was plain to hear.

"Connor is such a great kid, too. Kendra did a fabulous job raising him on her own." He was proud of his sister. She'd found herself pregnant and alone, thrown out of home, but she loved Connor and no sacrifice had been too great. He'd done everything he could to help her, and he had to admit he loved being an uncle to her children.

"That she did," said Stella, squeezing his knee under the table. "You were really there for her when your parents disowned her."

He'd wanted to kill the man who had knocked up his little sister and left her on her own with no money or protection. When he found out it was his business partner, Tom, it had almost cost them their friendship, but when he'd learned Tom never knew he had a son, and wanted to marry Kendra because he loved her, it had been a good day.

"So, when are you heading home?" Kade asked.

He didn't miss a beat or look at Stella. "I'm staying on for a few days."

Kade winked. "Funny. So is Stella."

There was a brief silence. "You told him?" Stella scolded Lexie.

Lexie held up her hand and wiggled her ring finger. "Married now. No secrets."

Stella sighed and addressed Kade. "It's not like that. We'll be friends without the benefits."

"Yeah, right," Kade laughed.

"What? I can be friends with a woman without sex being on the table."

Kade's smile died. "I'm not saying that you can't, but it's obvious you two have chemistry. With both of you unattached, ending up in bed after holidaying together is a no brainer. You're just fooling yourself," he said, directing this comment to Stella.

It's exactly what Marcus hoped for.

Stella merely changed the subject and turned to Kade. "You mentioned you'd do a book signing at my event and donate the sales to the charity. That is so generous of you, but I was wondering if I could ask for more. How about you offer a critique of someone's unpublished manuscript? We could auction that off on the night of the dinner."

Marcus really admired Stella. She had a large trust fund, which meant she never had to work a day in her life, but she worked tirelessly on causes close to her heart. This year her annual charity ball was for a charity working with teens who were illiterate for many reasons.

"Oh God, really? A critique? What if the winner's book is rubbish?"

Lexie laughed. "Then tell it like it is. That's what an editor would do if they submitted it. Be constructive in your feedback. I'm sure they'd appreciate it."

"Great. I'll add that to the programme for the dinner." Stella turned to Marcus. "And you could offer something too, even if not at the auction. How about an apprenticeship to work at Bad Boy Autos? It's a job that someone who has trouble with literacy can still thrive in."

That was a great idea. They were so busy that the trained mechanics could do with some help. It also meant they'd be slower because they were teaching, but, after a few years, he'd end up with well-trained mechanics who could really contribute to his business.

"How about I offer three apprenticeships?"

"Really? That's fabulous. How should we decide who gets these positions?"

"How about we do a draw at the auction? We auction the right to draw one name out of a barrel. That way I can help raise money too as well as employing the three teens."

Her answering smile made his day. "That's an amazing idea. I can imagine how many people would love the chance to pay to draw a name that might change someone's life. Thank you." She pressed a kiss to his lips.

"Oh, no. None of that," Kade laughingly said.

"Isn't it time you two hit the road? Don't you have a flight to catch?" Marcus threw back at his so-called friend.

Lexie squealed and pushed her chair back. "We do. Come on, husband." She beamed with joy. "I love saying that."

After much hugging and kissing, and a few tears, the happy couple left. Stella sat back down. "How can you not want to have that?"

"I'd be terrible at it." There it was. He admitted his fear.

"Don't be ridiculous. Why do you think that?"

His back was bloody killing him and she wanted to have a heart to heart with a man who didn't have one. He slowly rose to his feet and offered her his arm. "Come on. You promised me a relaxing day at the spa. Sitting for too long really kills my back."

"Deflecting I see," she replied, but she rose and took his hand.

"Conversations like this need to be accompanied by copious amounts of alcohol and it's far too early for that."

CHAPTER SIX

The spa was a perfect hunting ground for a man like Marcus. Stella wished she could take back her words. She should never have admitted that Marcus wasn't her boyfriend when the young woman behind the reception desk asked if they wanted a couple's massage. Instead, she'd fallen into the trap.

So, here she was pasting a cheerful smile on her face and playing the 'friend card' even though she wanted to drag him away, as the ladies in the spa just about crawled all over him.

Not only did she have to contend with the beauticians panting after him, every woman in the spa suddenly sat up straighter, boobs out and lips pouting, as he beamed his sexy smile at them.

"A target rich environment for you," she whispered, as they were handed their robes.

"Hey, this was your idea, and correct me if I'm wrong, but you were the one to call off our arrangement. If you want to change your mind, I'm happy to oblige."

Her jealousy dimmed slightly at his offer, considering the place was full of beautiful, sexy women. "I'm good, thanks."

"If you'll follow me?"

"I'm so looking forward to this. What? My back's killing me," Marcus uttered, as he followed the beautician.

"You can get changed in the booth, and there is paper underwear for you to wear." She flashed a smile at Marcus, "naked is also fine."

"I just bet it is," Stella said to herself under her breath. How long would it be before she couldn't stop the claws from coming out?

However, as soon as she lay on the table, she felt the tension drain from her shoulders, until she saw Marcus emerge from the changing room. His towel sat low on his hips, exposing his tan line. There was no fat beneath the sun-kissed skin, just lean muscles that rippled as he walked. She forced her gaze a fraction higher, skimming over the dusting of masculine hair, the dark nipples. He had straight, broad shoulders and sleek, curving muscle stretching down his arms. He looked so fit and healthy that for a moment she forgot he was in constant pain.

She also remembered what it felt like to tangle in the sheets with his masculine perfection, and the craving made her mouth water.

Marcus sighed as soon as the massage started. Thankfully, with her head in the table hole, she didn't have to watch another woman running her hands across his naked skin, but her imagination tightened her gut.

"It's fine, just ignore the scars. They don't hurt." She heard Marcus tell his masseuse.

Stella rarely noticed his scars, but she could still remember seeing him in hospital. On her first visit, she at least knew he'd live. Just after the crash, while he lay in a hospital bed in Italy, no one knew if he'd live or die. For the first three weeks she'd barely slept. Unable to fly to his side, or show how much she was hurting, almost drove her mad. She had to sit back and comfort Kendra.

She should have stopped their relationship then, but he'd needed her, or so she'd told herself. Now it looked like he needed her again, or maybe she was fooling herself.

It was her that needed him.

"What shall we do for dinner?" She asked, to change the subject and because she wanted to spend time tonight finishing the conversation he'd deflected at lunch. Why did he think he would make a terrible husband and father?

He *was* a workaholic, but Stella thought that was because he had nothing else in his life to fill the void. He'd always been driven. You didn't get to be a world champion in anything without that, but Bad Boy Autos was also doing really well.

"I thought I'd have dinner in my room. I have some contracts I need to look over. Especially if we're spending the day on the water tomorrow."

"What sort of contracts?"

"Tom and I are thinking of expanding. There's an opportunity in Miami."

She'd heard nothing about that. Kendra hadn't mentioned expansion.

"Gosh, your latissimus dorsi are really, really tight. Is your back giving you pain? If so, and if you're under the care of a back specialist I'd get him to evaluate you." The young woman massaging said softly to Marcus.

Marcus wasn't lying about the pain, or the doctor's recommendation then. She couldn't hear Marcus's mumbled reply.

She waited for Marcus to say more about his expansion plans, but when nothing was given, she asked, "Miami? Sounds exciting. Who would manage the new branch?" As the silence lengthened, she rose up on her forearms to look at Marcus. "Who's going to run it?"

"It hasn't been decided yet. Tom and I have to determine if we think it's the right location and opportunity."

"And if you do?" She asked, as she lay back down on the table.

"Initially, either Tom or I will have to be based there until we're sure it's running how we need. Then we'll likely put a manager in."

Either option was terrible. She'd lose Kendra, Matti and Connor, or Marcus.

"How long would one of you have to be in Miami?"

"A year, maybe two at the most."

She knew who would end up going. "Kendra has mentioned nothing about moving. Does she know?"

"Yes. I think Tom and Kendra would like to stay in LA as Connor's ready for school here."

"So, what you're really saying is you'll be going to Miami."

"Probably."

"Roll over, Mr. Black." The masseuse didn't even turn away as he rolled, revealing more of his spectacular body to her. Her hackles rose.

This expansion information was delivered as if it wouldn't matter to her. With a start, as she rolled over too, she realized it *shouldn't* matter to her. She'd ended their relationship and was moving on.

"You mentioned contracts? Are you thinking of opening across the US?" No wonder Marcus didn't want to be tied to one woman. He wanted to build an empire. How could she have been so stupid? A world champion would never be satisfied with one successful chop shop.

"Not everywhere. I want to keep exclusivity, but probably New York and maybe Chicago."

She squeezed her eyes shut, and not just because the woman was digging into her thighs. Calling an end to their FWB was one thing, but realizing she'd never see him again was another.

Still, this is what she wanted. If he wasn't in LA, it should make it easier to move on. Shouldn't it? Out of sight, out of mind, so the saying goes.

Then why did the idea of never seeing him again hurt so much?

After the massages, they made their way to the gym and had a great workout.

"I'm going to finish with a swim before hitting work in my room. The cruise sets off at seven tomorrow morning. I'll meet you in the lobby at about 6.30am."

He'd blown her off. "So, I can't get room service with you?"

Marcus flicked a piece of hair off her face. "I don't think that's a good idea. I'm trying hard to behave and having you in my room with a bed right there would be too much of a temptation."

"You think I'd give into temptation?" She asked, already knowing that she probably would, especially after seeing him almost naked all afternoon.

He gave her one of his sexy, smoldering smiles, and her face flushed with color. He knew the answer to that, just as she did. He leaned over, pressed a kiss to her lips and automatically her mouth opened for him. His tongue swept in, and she wanted him to sweep her into his arms more than she wanted to breathe. He finally broke the kiss on a groan.

"I think we have our answer. If you're serious about ending our FWB arrangement, then I'll see you in the morning." His raised eyebrow indicated he was waiting for an answer, but she couldn't form any words. She was torn in two. Her heart yelled for her to go for it, while her head told her it would only break her heart when they got back to LA.

"I'll see you in the lobby tomorrow morning."

Marcus sighed, but he still smiled. As she quickly walked away, she heard him mumble, "She still wants me."

And she hated the fact she did.

THE NEXT MORNING, MARCUS MADE SURE HE WAS IN THE LOBBY early. He grabbed two coffees. Stella liked her coffee black, while he had to have cream and sugar.

He stood just inside the entrance to the resort hotel, directly across from the elevators, so he could watch her as she exited and walked toward him. He knew he could have pushed her yesterday. She was on the verge of agreeing to spend the night with him, but he'd promised he'd give the business in Miami an answer by the end of the week. He still had a few things he wanted to talk with Tom about. Besides, he would have her all to himself on the boat today.

Plus, nagging in the back of his mind was the situation with his back. His doctor was recommending surgery urgently before he did permanent damage to himself, that could mean a wheelchair for the rest of his life. He couldn't buy a business in Miami if he had to have surgery and Tom didn't want to go.

The doors to the elevators opened and he stood up straight. Stella. She wore a floaty skirt to her knees, with flat sandals and a white halter top that showed off her tan. Her hair was tied in a ponytail as usual and she wore huge sunglasses atop her head. She looked closer to eighteen than twenty-six and every head in the lobby turned to watch her walk towards him with her beach bag overflowing.

She's mine, his beaming smile said, and just to press home the point, he bent his head and gave her a kiss.

Once his audience had seen enough, he pulled back and handed her a coffee.

"Are you ready for a day of sun and fun?"

"Absolutely. Where are we going?"

He linked his arm through hers. "It's a surprise, but let's get moving. You know the wind always picks up in the afternoon."

He had a driver waiting, and soon they were heading to where the boat was moored.

"Did you get your work done?" she asked.

He leaned back in the seat and replied, "Yes. I have a few things to talk to Tom about but it's looking promising." Did he detect her mouth turn down at his response? "It's always best to have a second opinion."

She looked out the window. "I'll miss you if you go."

Why did that thought please him so much? "I haven't gone yet."

She turned to look at him and he swallowed hard at the look in her eyes. She looked lost, but she was the one who'd ended their relationship. *Because she wants more, asshole, and you can't give it to her, can't promise her that.*

They reached the marina and he led them to mooring 35. His beautiful launch, named Y-Knot, sat gleaming white with a blue shade sail at the back. Hani was here to ensure everything he'd organized was in place.

"Welcome back, Mr. Black. You're all fueled and ready to go. Your provisions are all loaded too. I'll meet you back here at around 3.30pm."

"Thanks, Hani. This is Stella Perry."

"Hi Hani. Do you trust this beauty with Marcus?"

"I have to. It's his boat."

Stella looked at him. "Booked a cruise, did you? Liar. Boys with toys once again."

Marcus laughed. "I bought it after I'd recovered from my accident. I needed a place to escape, to think about my future. Tom and I sailed around Maui for a few days and Bad Boy Autos was born." He reached for her hand. "Come on. I know you've sailed a lot so we'll manage fine."

Hani cast them off and they powered along the coast towards the Molokini crater. He had two kayaks on the back, and the galley was full of food and drink.

Stella was off exploring the boat and when she arrived back at the bridge, she had a beer in her hand. "You're driving so I brought a Coke for you."

He took it, not wanting to admit he'd taken a pill or two this morning.

"Y-Knot is stunning. How many does it sleep?"

"There are two ensuite cabins and one other berth that sleeps four in bunks with a bathroom."

"Do you use it very often?"

"Not really, but I think Tom will use it with Kendra and the kids."

Stella sat back in the chair next to him and sighed. "So, what's the plan? You told me you'd booked a cruise?"

"I had to book a slot at the crater. They can't have every boat in that space so you pay for a slot. We have from 8am to 10am. Then I thought we'd cruise further up the coast and find a spot to snorkel or kayak."

"I have always wanted to go to the Molokini crater. I hope we see some turtles."

"I hope so too. I haven't been there either."

She stared at him open-mouthed, then stuttered, "You own this boat but haven't been to the crater?"

"I've never had anyone I wanted to share the experience with." He observed her face. She looked away, but not before he saw her lips turn up.

Stella tried not to let her heart soar. He'd always been a smooth talker when it came to the ladies.

"It's about another half hour before we get there."

She studied his profile while he was busy looking at the instruments. He looked relaxed, but she noted the tightening in his mouth every time he bent to look at the navigation.

"Since we have some time, why don't you tell me what the doctor is really saying about your back."

To her surprise, it wasn't anger scoring Marcus's mouth it was fear and her stomach fell.

"There isn't much to tell."

She watched him closely for a moment. "I think there is. They won't allow you to stay on the pills for too long, and it's obvious you can't function without them. Your pupils are pin pricks. How many pills did you take this morning?"

"Two, but I'm not high."

"Did you bring them with you?" He ran a hand through his hair and now it was anger scoring his mouth. "Don't tell me it's none of my business, because I'm on a boat with you in the middle of the ocean."

"I didn't bring them with me and you can check my stuff. The swimming should help my back."

She nodded. "If you don't want to share what the doctor is saying, tell me why you'd make a terrible husband and father."

He laughed and looked across at her as if to say, *you don't know?*

"My father. I'm just like my father. Driven, arrogant, selfish"
—

"Don't be ridiculous. You are those things, but that doesn't make you like your father. You're kind and generous, you're respectful of other people's views and you, unlike your father, understand the definition of family. Look what you did for Kendra."

When he said nothing more, she added, "I think you'd make a brilliant father. I've seen you with Connor. You love that little boy." She considered him for a long moment.

He turned to look at her. "What?"

"I think you'd love to be a father, but you're scared; scared of failure, scared of being hurt. That's what is stopping you from admitting you too would like to find Mrs. Right."

"That's not what I'm afraid of…" That made her sit up, but before she could probe further, he slowed the boat. "We're here." He cut the engine and made his way to the lower deck to drop the anchor.

She looked at the beautiful, blue sparkling water and cursed. He wasn't afraid of being a father, so he was afraid of…what? *Think, girl.* Perhaps he feared becoming a part-time father if the relationship didn't last. She knew what growing up in a broken home was like, but then again, her parents were never parents in the true sense of the word.

She stood up and made her way down to join him. She had all afternoon to find out and she slipped off her skirt and pulled her top over her head to reveal her skimpy G-string bikini. That ought to get Marcus's blood heating and his brain fuddled.

CHAPTER SEVEN

"I thought we'd go snorkeling first to see if the turtles are there, then we can go k—holy shit." Marcus stopped dead as he saw her. Her plan seemed to work. "You are hot."

She walked to his side. She wasn't playing fair, letting her hips sway a bit, and took the snorkeling gear from his hand. "Let's go then." She looked down. "The cool water might help your hard on."

"I know a better way to help my hard on," he said, and reached for her, but Stella was already clambering over the side. She smiled at his groan.

They snorkeled for about half an hour. There were plenty of turtles, and she loved every minute. The volcano reef was like submerging herself into another world. Finally, she knew it was time to head back to the boat, dry off and warm up. When she reached the boat, Marcus was already on board, and he offered his hand to pull her out of the water but she brushed it aside to clamber on board and into his arms without putting further strain on his back.

The heat his body generated matched that of the sun, and for one long minute she let herself feel it. She closed her eyes as his lips brushed down her neck, and she shivered. She didn't stop him as his lips went lower or as he bent her over his arm. He nuzzled her bikini top aside and latched on to one hard nipple, and this time it was she who groaned. His nimble fingers quickly undid her wet top, and it fell to the deck. She should stop him, but she really didn't want to.

He led her to the privacy of the lounger under the shade sail at the back of the boat and lay her down, away from any eyes on boats that may speed past. He stood, staring at her, his eyes like fingers as they traversed her bare skin.

"You're so beautiful." The longing in his words soothed her fears. "What is it about you, that I can't let you go?"

Read nothing into that. Be in the moment—this perfect moment. "You make me feel beautiful." She rose to her elbows. "Is your back up to this?"

"Every part of me is up for this."

She laughed.

He didn't join her as she expected. "I haven't changed my mind, Stella. I'm not looking for permanent. If you're okay with that then I'll be all over you."

Now she understood how Marcus felt when looking at his pill bottle. You knew it was bad for you, but you just had to have it. "I don't want to be FWB again but I suppose we could have a Hawaiian fling?"

A dazzling smile broke across Marcus's face. "I like the way you're thinking. What happens in Maui stays in Maui."

She reached up and ran a finger down his bare chest. "A final goodbye." Maybe a last fling would give her closure. *Bullshit, you know it's an excuse.*

Marcus needed no further encouragement. He'd fantasized about this for months. Had it been that long since he'd made love with Stella? It felt like an eternity. He took a deep breath to steady his eagerness, or it would be over too soon. The things he wanted to do…

He knew this was a gift he probably didn't deserve, but he'd been honest. He couldn't offer her more, and once she learned his prognosis, she'd likely not want him, anyway. Damaged goods didn't make great lovers, husbands or fathers. How could he encumber Stella, a socialite with the world at her feet, and a great love of life, with a man who might end up in a wheelchair?

She was watching him, a knowing look in her eyes. "I won't expect more, I promise. I know you too well."

He shrugged. "That's what I adore about you. You know the real me and still want to be with me." He stripped off his shorts and moved over her, lifted a hand to stroke her cheek. He leaned forward and gently caught her lower lip between his teeth. She murmured her approval. He sucked on it, let his tongue run over the swell of her pout. She had lips that made a man think of how good they would feel around his cock. The memory set his blood on fire.

"If this is my last time with you, I will not rush it. I want to savor every inch of you." He traced her collarbone with his fingers and loved how Stella's pupils widened and her breath grew ragged. Her open response to him always turned him on. He pressed a kiss to her cheek. She turned her head, but he didn't take her sweet mouth. Instead, he let his lips nibble on the skin below her ear, before gently biting on the soft lobe. Her shiver was intoxicating.

She moved restlessly under him, each movement sending his heightened senses spiraling. He hung his head, trying to regain control above his pounding need to take her. That was difficult, given the sight of her bare breasts and hardened nipples. He wanted to taste them more than he wanted his next breath.

He ran his lips across the tanned skin of her throat. He felt her pulse beating beneath his mouth, could almost taste her subtle scent that he found so sexy. Her head fell back, giving him access to anything he wanted to take, and he gloried in this offering.

He wouldn't be rushed, but the strain of control was slipping. He carried on to the slopes of her breasts and finally found one hardened nipple. When it slipped between his lips, he sighed.

Her hands lifted to entwine around his neck. "Marcus." The raw need in her voice thrilled him. "I hate to stop you but condom?"

"Don't be in such a hurry. For what I have in mind we don't need one—yet. Besides, I'll need more than one."

"Promises, promises," she sighed as her hips lifted, circling, pushing into him in that way that would soon drive him out of his mind with need. To stop her talking, he once more took her nipple between his teeth and gave a light bite. He couldn't resist suckling harder, until she cried out his name.

Slowly he made his way down her body, kissing each rib along the way. She giggled. He knew how ticklish she was, so he took his time, loving the throaty sounds she made. This would not be a quickie. He wanted her every which way he could have her. To imprint on his memory just how wonderful they were together. He was going to imprint himself on every part of her.

Stella looked down her body at the man worshipping it with his lips and tongue. His touch was demanding, yet reverent. She wanted to watch but that sensual mouth, those full lips brushing against her, set her body on fire and she could barely take the torture.

Impatience tore through her, and she tilted her hips toward him, silently begging him to taste her. Finally, she sucked in a breath as he used his teeth to pull down her skimpy bikini bottom. She lifted her butt to help him. She lay back, eyes closed, savoring his scent and waited for his tongue to send her over the edge, but it never came.

Her eyes flew open and connected with his. He concentrated his gaze on her face, of all places, considering she lay naked before him. A feast for his eyes. Were the hormones bouncing so hard, or was that a look of longing she saw written on his face?

Not breaking eye contact with her, he slowly lowered his head and...he licked her. "You taste like ambrosia. I could eat you all day."

God, she wanted to come.

She could not look away as his tongue swirled, tasted, teased her most intimate, most sensitive part. She wouldn't last long. Unashamedly thrusting her pelvis into him, she rode him like a cowgirl. Waves of pleasure built. The waves rose higher, faster; she willed them to wash her away on a tide of orgasms. She could feel the heat of his mouth so close to her, she thought she would die of pleasure.

Would she ever stop wanting him? She didn't want to look into her heart, but the heat for him burned deep inside. Would the fire of desire ever die? She reached out and drove her hands into his thick, vibrant hair. She pulled him close. Her back arched, tension locking her body in an endless moment of togetherness. His hands tugged at her thighs as he pushed them wider so his hungry mouth could go deeper, suck harder and nip until she thought she really would die.

And he didn't stop.

It was as if he couldn't get enough of her.

The rhythm switched from slow to fast, hard to soft, and it drove her crazy. Her body burst with a shower of rainbow colors behind her eyes. She fell back as she shook; her cry high and harsh and long.

Still, he didn't stop, giving no respite. Instead, his clever mouth forced every ripple of response from her until neither body or mind could focus on anything but the mindless pleasure pulsing through every cell in her body.

As Stella lay there, trying to hold on to the incredible feelings, Marcus's hands traced across her. Gentle kisses fluttered on her stomach, her chest, to her face, where he took her lips in a gentle, yet possessive kiss.

Her pulse slowed, her breathing steadied, until he bent and whispered in her ear, "Never forget." Her eyes flew open, and her heart followed. He lifted his head from her skin, and she willed him to meet her gaze. She *would* never forget, and that might just cost her everything.

Then he was gone and she knew the loss she felt now was nothing like the loss she'd feel when they got back to LA. She'd feel a world of pain, but that didn't stop her from wanting him inside her.

He was back before she'd considered moving, a roll of condoms in his hand. "You're optimistic," she said, with a smile.

"Let's see shall we?"

"How's your back? Perhaps you should take a seat."

Marcus's sexy smile grew as he sat on one of the high stools and twirled around. His cock hard as rock and pointing, long and thick, halfway up his stomach. "You know me so well." He looked kind of comical, sexy comical, spinning on the stool, as naked as the day he was born. After a few turns, he slowed and beckoned her with his finger. What woman could resist this masculine picture of perfection? She sure as hell couldn't.

Limbs still lethargic, from the fabulous orgasm he'd given her, finally moved, and she pushed to her feet. He watched her walk toward him like a starving man looking at a feast through the window. Longing and need, and something else she wouldn't consider, evident on his face. Her heart gave an extra beat. He was so easy to love.

This time it was her turn to take the lead. This time it was she who pushed his legs apart so she could stand between them. His rock-hard abs just begged to be kissed, and she leaned in and pressed her lips to his heated skin. No other part of her touched him. Just her lips. She trailed them lower, but suddenly two hands gripped her. "Later. I want to be inside you. Clamber up." She used the steering wheel, if that is what it is called, to pull herself up until she was astride two strong, muscled thighs. He spread his legs so she was wide open to him and his hand slipped between her legs.

"I love how wet you are for me."

She shuddered as he found her hardened nub, still so sensitive from his mouth. Sex was where they were in perfect unison. Why couldn't he see that there could be so much more than sex between them. They were already best friends and they knew each other's weaknesses and strengths.

She used the stools foot bars to raise herself and she impatiently patted his hand away so she could slide down the hard length of him. She loved the feel of him inside, not too big and definitely not small. He was just perfect and she loved how he made her body come alive.

She smiled at him as she rose slowly and slid back down, hanging on to his broad shoulders. Her eyes widened as he used his hands to lift her and slide her down over and over to impale her on his hard length. Even though he raged with the need to possess her, wanted to drive into her, Marcus held back and let her take the lead.

He held her tightly against him and gave her a hard, demanding kiss while he let her body adjust to him. She was just as hot and tight as he remembered and he'd never encountered another woman who made him feel the way she did. With care, he lifted her up and brought her back down, just a little further than the last time.

Exquisite sensation sizzled along his skin and he devoured her lips, biting and sucking them until Stella grew restless. She tightened her thighs, lifting up and wrapping her arms around his neck.

Suddenly, she broke the kiss and stared into his eyes. "I can never get enough of you. Make love to me."

THE CHANGE THAT CAME OVER MARCUS'S FACE ENTHRALLED Stella. His eyes darkened to charcoal and his jaw clenched. Gone was the teasing man, replaced by an intense version of the man she loved. The storm of passion that had been brewing between them this weekend swept over them as he got a firmer hold on her and began following her order.

"The pleasure is all mine," he ground out between his clenched teeth. "I could do this all day."

"Promises. Promises."

He completely filled her, making her wild for the kind of pleasure that only Marcus could give her. Her desire for him was unquenchable and she knew that even though they were making love now, she'd want him again almost immediately.

Those powerful arms of his lifted and lowered her easily as she held onto him. Their eyes locked as they started moving in time with each other. Always in tune in their passion. Every thrust sent them higher along the climb to the summit.

Stella's heart raced even faster when Marcus growled and gripped her buttocks harder. "I'm not going to hold out long. It's too good, too incredible and I've been without you for far too long."

She shook her head. "It doesn't matter. I've missed you so much. I'm ready."

Immediately, his tempo increased and his jaw tensed as her pace matched his. Their rhythm grew almost frantic in their quest for fulfilment. It was even hotter than in the past and every nerve in her body was centered on where they were connected. He was long and thick and she wanted all of him.

She tightened her legs around him, raising up and coming down harder, taking him to the hilt. Their bodies slapped together as Marcus's thrusts grew in power.

Stella grasped his shoulders tighter as her release began. "Oh, God. Yes. Don't stop."

"I won't. I can't. Not now." His voice was hoarse. "Come for me, Stella. I want to feel you come."

The pulses in her centre became more intense as he repeatedly drove into her. Suddenly, she soared over the edge, held prisoner by the sheer ecstasy that crashed over her. She screamed his name and hugged him close, hanging on as the undulating waves of her climax threatened to sweep her away.

CHAPTER EIGHT

Stella repeatedly clenched around him, and his control snapped. Her scream of pleasure sent him over the precipice.

"Oh, Stella," he said. "It's been far too long."

He rocketed into an orgasm that robbed him of his breath for several moments. His back arched forward a little as he exploded inside her but even the sharp stab of pain couldn't diminish his pleasure. Reasonable thought left him as he spilled his seed and let out a few raspy groans. It seemed to go on forever and he wouldn't have minded a bit if it had.

But finally the storm of passion began to abate and he relaxed his grip on Stella's spectacular ass. Leaning forward, he kissed her thoroughly, drawing her tongue into his mouth and sucking on it.

When the kiss ended, he met her gaze. "Without a doubt, no one has ever made me feel as good as you do. I swear. Why are we walking away from this friends with benefits thing again?"

"You know why. Don't try and get me in my weakened moment to change my mind. I want more, and you can't or won't give me that."

For one moment he wanted to say yes. He wanted to say I could give you more but then his back spasmed and he knew now was not the time to try to change his ways. He'd only end up hurting his best friend.

A FEW HOURS LATER, TRUE TO HIS BOAST, THEY'D USED MOST OF the condoms he'd earlier acquired. They'd had to be careful of his back but he'd told her the pain wasn't that bad. The last bout of love making had been plain old missionary position, but he never made it feel plain, or boring. She loved the weight of his hard body atop her. She was replete but, like an addict, eager for more. Perhaps his back wasn't as bad as she'd previously thought.

"That was quite the sendoff. The boat was rocking and not from the waves."

She swallowed back her reply that it *was* mind-blowingly amazing, the best she'd ever had, or was likely to ever have again and that he'd spoiled her for any other man, wanted to scream from her lips.

"What happens in Maui stays in Maui, right?" She tried to make her conversation light so he wouldn't know she was dying inside. Why couldn't he see they were perfect together? She wasn't looking for Mr. Right, because she'd found him.

Mr. Right was in front of her.

He lay on his side, facing her, running his fingers down her arm. She could tell he wanted to say something, but she couldn't understand what held him back. Fear of commitment? That couldn't be it. He'd committed to becoming the formula world champion. He'd committed to building Bad Boy Autos. He'd stood by his sister when her family disowned her and he'd stood by his friend when he had every reason not to.

Why couldn't he commit to her?

What was he so afraid of?

"You wear no jewelry." His finger ran round her ring finger. "With the size of your trust fund you should be dripping in diamonds."

She blew her fringe out of her eyes. "I'm not a jewelry kind of girl, but I can't say that about shoes."

"You never flash your cash. I like that about you. Do you still drive that old VW? Money, and the trappings of wealth don't impress you do they?"

"Money doesn't make you happy."

He rose to his elbow, cradling his head with his hand as he studied her. "I'm glad not everyone is like you or Bad Boy Autos would be in serious trouble."

"Don't get me wrong. I like money. It gives me freedoms most people don't have, but with it comes responsibility to help those less fortunate than myself."

He sighed. "Sometimes I think you're too good to be true."

"Don't do that. Don't put me on a pedestal. You'll be disappointed."

He laughed. "Disappointed? Hardly. You make me so pleased I'm a hot-blooded male." He bent to place his lips on her stomach, when suddenly he let out a blood curdling scream and crumpled onto his back. "Fuck me, that hurts." He rolled to his side, clutching his back. "I need my pills or I won't be able to get us home."

She quickly pulled a cushion off the lounger and placed it so he could try to roll onto it.

"Don't touch, please, don't touch me."

"What can I do?" She hated seeing anyone in pain, but to see a man so big and strong like Marcus, writhing in agony broke her heart.

"Pills."

"I thought you said you didn't bring them."

"Fuckin' hell. I didn't."

"I have some Tylenol in my bag. I'll get it."

"And some ice. My back feels like it's on fire."

She hurried to help. She got a glass of water and the Tylenol first, then ran back to the galley for ice. She wrapped it in a hand towel and raced to where Marcus lay in pain. She gently put it against his back as he lay on his side with his eyes closed and his teeth clenched.

"Your back is much worse than you've let on, isn't it? You should have brought the pills with you. I had no right to accuse you of being addicted to them." She blinked back the tears. She caused this. She shouldn't have stuck her nose in, as if she knew it all. Her mother's addiction clouded her view.

"I *am* addicted, but only because the pain is so bad. I'm sure if my back wasn't fucked I could walk away from them."

Could he? He did have a will of iron. "You can't go on like this. What does the doctor say?"

"I have to have more surgery."

"Then why haven't you had it"

"It's not that simple."

Then it hit her. She remembered when he'd had surgery for his back after the accident. They'd explained there was a risk he might wake up paralyzed or certainly never able to walk again. Was the risk the same? She lay down next to him on the bare deck. "The risk."

He lay there with his eyes closed, his lips white. She stroked his face, pushing his hair out of his eyes.

She wanted to say the right thing, but she didn't know what that was. It would sound flippant. She wasn't the one facing life as a cripple, or worse. But someone had to be sensible. "You've never been one to hide from the truth. I don't think you have a choice."

He opened his eyes and looked at her. "I know, but I wanted to put it off for as long as I could and enjoy life for a bit longer. Enjoy you," he whispered.

"This isn't enjoyment. It's agony."

"The morning has been the most beautiful of days. I want more time with you."

"This is only on Maui. There is no us. You and I don't want the same things from life."

He opened his mouth and shut it again.

They lay side by side on the deck, Stella holding his hand, the waves gently lapping the boat, rocking them as if they were babies needing comfort. They couldn't stay like this all day.

She stood. "I'll take us back to the dock. Hopefully, the Tylenol will be enough to get you back to the hotel and get you home. You need to see Dr. Forrester."

Marcus tried to move, and groaned. "Are you sure you can handle the launch?"

Not arguing with her was a bad sign. The pain must be bad. "No, but I'll only find out if I try. I've driven boats before, just not this big.

"I'll phone Hani. He can meet the boat and help you dock, or maybe I'll be fine by the time we reach the dock and I can take her in."

She looked at him, lying on the deck, his mouth tight with pain, his face white. "You don't need to be a hero. Here's a bottle of water. Don't move. If you need help to move or anything else, call for me."

She was about to start the engine, but made a call first. She had coverage this close to shore. When she finally got hold of Dr. Forrester, she told him what had happened. He advised her not to move Marcus. He'd organize an ambulance to meet them at the dock. Dr. Forrester would arrange for someone at Kula Hospital to assess his condition. Then they could decide if it was safe for Marcus to fly home.

She took a deep breath. "I hope I'm not overreacting?"

"No. You're doing the right thing. Hopefully, it's only a

prolapsed disc that can be helped with treatment like physiotherapy and rest. He's had them before."

"What if it isn't?" She held her breath. "He told me you've
recommended more surgery."

"I can't really discuss Marcus's situation with you. Let's just
get him stabilized, out of pain and back in LA as soon as
possible."

"I can do that."

"Thank you for calling me. I wish Marcus took his condition
as seriously as you obviously do."

CHAPTER NINE

Hospitals sucked and being in the hospital in Maui sucked harder. Thank God for Stella.

Marcus tried to be a good patient, but he had no patience and being told to lie still and not move for three days was his version of hell.

"How's Mr. Grumpy this morning?"

Stella stood in the doorway, and of course the young intern, Andy, was right behind her. He was never around when Marcus wanted to talk about his case, but was in his room when Stella was here. Andy couldn't take his eyes off Stella, but he better keep his hands off her or he'd... he'd do what? Stand up and fight the jerk? Fall down in a heap with pain?

"I'd feel better if you came here and gave me a kiss." Take that Dr. Randy Andy.

"I'm sure I could arrange something," Stella said, as she leaned down and pressed a lingering kiss to his lips. He wished he could pull her onto the bed with him. She smelled good enough to eat.

Stella pulled back and stroked his fringe out of his eyes. "I've got some news. I've organized a private plane with a nurse to fly us back to LA."

"What would I do without you?"

He loved her smile. "Speaking of what would you do," she paused and looked over her shoulder at Andy. "The Doc here says you'll need some help at home."

He flashed the Doc a look. Where was the guy going with this? Was he trying to make Marcus look like a helpless dick in front of Stella? Point out to her why she'd be best to run a mile?

"So," she said, and bit her bottom lip. Not a good sign. "Andy suggested getting a live-in helper, but I thought perhaps you'd be more comfortable with me coming to stay."

Ha! Andy's face didn't like that suggestion. Good. Did he want Stella in his house? While his body loved the idea, his head screamed that it would be a mistake. Something was happening between them and while he would love to have Stella in his house and in his bed, she wanted something he couldn't give her.

She wanted forever, with Mr. Right.

He was so far from being Mr. Right. The dream she had in her head of having a family and a white picket fence would never come true if she stayed with him.

But if it could be forever… for some reason that idea didn't suck the breath from his lungs until he thought he'd curl up and die. Not when forever could be with her. Could he offer her what she really wanted?

Was he being a total dick? There were plenty of men and women who lived in wheelchairs. Some even had children, and loving partners.

They weren't him. He remembered what a bastard he'd become when his racing career ended. He'd jumped at the chance to fill himself and those around him with self-pity. What would a selfish bastard like him do if he wound up in a wheelchair?

That wasn't what was making his body fill with fear as if he'd swallowed a cement mixer. There was a chance he'd end up impotent. He'd lose the main thing he loved about being a man. Sex was his world most days and nights. As it was to Stella.

There had to be more between them than great sex if he had any hope of a relationship lasting should the worst happen.

Tell her. Tell her the worst. Then see if she wants a relationship.

But what did 'coming to stay' mean? Platonic? Friends with benefits again? Or was this Stella's way of making him try for more? Did she even want a relationship with him? If she was looking for Mr. Right, then presumably she'd already decided he wasn't it. Did he want to be her Mr. Right?

Don't be ridiculous. How could you be with a failing body?

He said, "Do you mind, Doc? I think we need some privacy."

Andy wasn't happy, but he left, and the door closed softly behind him.

He turned to look at Stella and she pushed on before he could stop her. "I know what you think. That this is a bad idea. However, now that friends with benefits is over and we are just friends, why can't one friend help another?"

Every fiber in his being told him this was a terrible idea. Stella gave him mixed signals. One minute she no longer wanted to share his bed, said their FWB should end and the next she's staying in Maui and having fantastic sex with him on his boat. He doubted if she moved in that they could stay just friends.

"Admit it. You'll need help. Would you prefer someone you don't know? Or is there someone else you'd prefer living with you?"

Now that was a loaded question. He cupped her cheek with his hand. "If I had anyone moving in to look after me, it would be you or Kendra, but as I don't want Kendra to know how bad this has become…"

"And here I thought you'd be all 'we could never just be

friends.'" It wasn't said with a smile. In fact, it almost sounded like an accusation.

"In case you haven't noticed, I'm not really in any condition to offer any benefits to the friends part."

Her smile was back. "True. Does this mean you agree?"

"What about your charity work? I know the ball is in three weeks. I don't want you pushing aside all your hard work for me."

She waved a hand. "Don't worry about that. I can do most of the work from your home. I may have to pop out for a few meetings or better yet, they can come to me at your place. Carey Stevenson is doing most of the operational tasks. I'm organizing raffles and providing the celebrity guest list."

Carey Stevenson? Marcus knew him. They'd customized a Maserati for him about eight months ago. He was the son of a famous rock musician who'd had a few hit records with a boy band in his youth and he was a real player. Was he taking Marcus's place in the FWB area? A stab of something akin to pain struck his chest. The green-eyed monster with a trident. Great. Just what he needed, pangs of jealousy to add to his pain overload.

Was it the green-eyed monster that made him say, "Just so we're clear, this is a strictly friends gig. We stick to your no more FWB plan." Stella's face was like a flashing billboard, so easy to read. "I agree with you about needing to end this relationship. You deserve to find what it is you want out of life and me... I'm happy with my life. I don't want it to change."

"You're happy with the back pain."

He laughed. "No, but I like my life. I have expansion plans for the business. Now is not the time to have a committed relationship, especially as I've never had one before. I'd be shit at it. Too selfish."

She shrugged. "That's the second time you've said that, and I think you're wrong, but I'm moving in because you, my stubborn man, need help. I'd hope you'd do the same for me if I needed it."

Would he? He looked at her and realized he wasn't as selfish as he thought, because he would do anything to help her.

"Surprised yourself, did you? You helped Kendra, and you helped Lexie, even when she was married to Jason. You might have this tough guy exterior but deep inside you have a soft spot for people, especially those in trouble."

He wasn't going to openly agree, but he knew he liked helping those who couldn't help themselves. Those whose life made them powerless for many reasons. For years he'd felt powerless against his father until one day he realized he was bigger and stronger and capable of making it on his own. Underdogs needed someone on their side. He'd never forget that feeling of powerlessness. Hell, he felt it now, knowing nothing he could do would fix his back.

"When can we leave?"

Stella shook her head. "Avoid much? I'll see about getting your discharge papers sorted, and we can be on our way. I've already collected your belongings from the hotel."

"By the way, no telling anyone about what has happened with my back. Not Kendra and Tom. No one." Stella's luscious lips formed a thin line and he waited because her silence was not an agreement. "Promise me."

"I think you should tell them. They deserve to know."

He laid back and closed his eyes. He'd tell them when he knew what he wanted to do. He didn't want anyone else pressurizing him. This was his life, the rest of his life. He'd decide regarding surgery when he was good and ready.

"I need space to assess things. Kendra will come barreling in and take over. This has to be my decision, because if anything goes wrong I—I know I'll try to blame someone."

She nodded thoughtfully. "I can understand that." She bent and gave him a brief kiss. "I'm always here if you want to talk and I promise I won't tell anyone about how bad your back is." As she stood in the doorway to his room she said, "But you best think up some story about why I'm moving in, because that's going to cause quite the stir. The player having a woman move in. Kendra and most everyone else, doesn't know about our FWB arrangement."

Once she'd gone to sort out the paperwork, Marcus lay still. No one would believe he had asked Stella to move in as his girl-friend. He was still pondering what they would say and suspect when Stella arrived with the nurse and paper work.

He hated that he was wheeled out of the hospital to a waiting car, and wheeled onto a plane, in a chair, but as they got him comfortable on the plane, Stella said, "I've already set up a plan. I've organized to have my apartment painted and you've kindly let me move in while it's being completed."

"You didn't have to do that. Did it need painting?"

"It did, and Kendra and I talked colors only a couple of weeks ago so she won't be suspicious, but she might think it's odd I'm staying with you. So, I had a further idea. I'll tell her I'm staying with you to talk you into providing a car for the charity auction. She'll believe that."

Another problem solved. "Thanks, Stella. I'll give you a car to auction. Hell, I'll talk to Damien at Porsche Orange County and get him to give a car too."

She threw her arms around his neck. "You are so wonderful. I wish you would see what I see."

His body roared to life, holding the sexy as hell woman in his arms, except she wasn't as close as he wanted because of the damn wheelchair. With a start he grasped that this could be his life in the very near future and determinedly pushed himself into a standing position, Stella helping him.

He clung to her, and not just for support. Her fragrance filled his senses, and her soft curves beckoned. He placed his lips to her neck, and her pulse slammed beneath his mouth. He shouldn't want her like this, but hell, he was a hot-blooded man and she always got him hot and bothered. He wanted her. He was pretty sure she could feel how much.

It was Stella who pulled back. "I'm not after a fling anymore, Marcus. I'm almost painting the nursery, and you're a lifetime away from wanting to commit to anyone. I'm here to help with your back and anything that comes from that. I can't be pulled back and forth and I can't be a convenience while you recuperate."

Guilt hit like a freight train. She was right. That wasn't fair to her. It seemed he wasn't about to buy cake and eat it too.

"Sorry, it won't happen again."

As she turned to lead him to the bed, his body tightened further as he saw the sad smile dying on her lips.

CHAPTER TEN

Stella had settled into Marcus's spare room happily. It was large and had a marvelous view of the sea. The bathroom was enormous, complete with a jet tub. It was like staying in a five-star hotel, except for the lack of room service.

She had the use of his office because he wasn't up to sitting in a hard chair or working for very long. When he did work he stood at the kitchen bench. Stella had ordered him a Varidesk that sat atop the bench, and he enjoyed working in the kitchen. It made it easier to get refreshments, and he could watch her cook.

The physiotherapist came daily and within a week he could manage limited movement on his four pain pills a day. He was back walking small distances but couldn't sit for very long.

With his limited mobility, she'd been able to avoid seeing too much of him, but she wished he wouldn't walk around all day with no top on and a pair of sweats that hung low on his hips. Okay, maybe she loved him walking around like this. She could see every drool worthy muscle in his chest, right down to his hips, leading into the out-of-bounds zone. She was obviously a woman who loved being teased because she hadn't once told him to put a t-shirt on.

She'd got back into cooking, though, something she found quite enjoyable. Marcus insisted on takeout for the first few nights, but she liked the thinking space cooking gave her. Plus, she needed to watch her carbs if she was to fit the dress she'd bought for the charity ball. The event was running smoothly. Carey was very good at his job, and most of her work was already done, with only a few more prizes to line up before the brochure was finalized.

When Friday arrived, the day the cleaner came so she could keep an eye on Marcus should he have a fall or anything, Stella kept her usual appointment for lunch with the girls. Catherine, the office manager at Bad Boy Autos, and Kendra were already at the restaurant when she arrived. Lexie was, of course, still on her honeymoon.

She'd barely had time to sit, order a drink and look at the menu before the cat got let out of the bag.

"Kendra didn't know you've been staying with Marcus." Damn. How did…

"I found out because I needed him to sign a few papers. He had them couriered to his house rather than have to come into the office. I heard you call out when I was on the phone with him. It suddenly became clear why he's playing hooky."

Kendra's face looked like it could start a war. "Don't be ridiculous. I'm staying there because my house is being painted. At the wedding I mentioned about trying to find a place and he offered me his spare room."

Kendra's rain cloud look vanished as if the sun had come out. "You could have come to ours."

"I need some peace as work is manic. The ball is only two weeks away." She let out a half breath when Kendra seemed to accept her rationale.

"Why did you stay longer in Hawaii? Marcus did too."

Catherine had that smirky smile on her face that said you're not fooling anyone. Stella wanted to kick her under the table.

"Marcus worked out I was stressed and suggested I stay. I said it wasn't much fun holidaying on your own so he agreed to keep me company."

"So good of him," Catherine smirked. Kendra luckily didn't bat an eyelid. Stella furiously said with her eyes 'back off' to Catherine.

"I hope you're both ready for the ball." Time to get her own back. "Who are you bringing as your date, Catherine?" Her friend didn't even hesitate.

"If you must know Carey's asked me."

Kendra gasped. "Oh, Catherine, he's a worse player than my brother." Catherine snorted and Kendra added, "Well, Marcus is. I love him to bits, and he's always been so good to me, but I despair that he'll ever get married. I think my parents' marriage really fucked with him and marriage is a noose that he'll not willingly step into. I get the impression that Carey is the same."

"But he's smokin' hot and probably great in bed. Sometimes a girl just wants a few orgasms and nothing more. Nothing serious." Catherine turned to Stella. "You'll back me up, right?"

"What I think is, it's the ladies' choice. If you're not looking for happy ever after then why not indulge in something just for pleasure?"

"The happy ever after is so much better. Believe me, I know." Kendra sat there with her smug smile and Stella wondered if her face had turned green with all the envy.

"But you have to get the right person if you're spending forever with them. What if you never find that?"

"Exactly," said Catherine. "Or you've found him and he doesn't feel the same."

The two single women threw a look at each other. Had Catherine met someone that she could picture forever with? Shit, she hoped it wasn't Marcus for a myriad of reasons. The main one being she couldn't bear to see Marcus with her friend. It would end their friendship. She wasn't that strong.

"I won't be flippant and say there's plenty more fish in the sea, but Lexie is a prime example of how you can discover someone."

Kendra was right. What looked on paper to be a disaster was something wonderful. Falling in love with your brother-in-law was a risk, but Lexie was brave enough to recognize what she wanted and needed. Why couldn't she be brave enough to tell Marcus how she felt? *Because Kade was the marrying kind and Marcus just isn't.*

"Perhaps it's because Stella and I fall for the wrong type of men; rich, arrogant and selfish."

"Yeah. Why do we do that?" She smiled at her friend, really wishing she knew.

"You're mixing with the wrong crowd. These men with more money than sense, have egos the size of Mt. Everest. They lead such busy lives they have no time for anyone but themselves."

"That's a bit harsh," she muttered. "Marcus has time for those he cares about and Carey too. I've seen no one work as hard as he has for my charity ball. I couldn't have done it without him."

"I know both men aren't as bad as I make them out to be, but there's a reason you never see either of them with a steady partner. They aren't the marrying kind."

"I suppose only time will tell," Catherine said. "And in the meantime, there is fun to be had."

MARCUS FINISHED HIS STRETCHES FOR THE DAY AND HEADED TO the shower. He'd followed his physio's orders like a good boy, and he had to admit it was helping. The pinched nerve was still there, but at least he could move without being in agony. The two pills in the morning and two at night worked at the moment, but for how long? He couldn't do anything strenuous without being back to square one. How could he drive a car, play golf, make love? Shit, that was scary, but so was having an operation which might destroy his life completely.

Once showered, he went to the kitchen to make some lunch, only to find Stella had left macaroni cheese in the fridge. He'd almost forgotten Connor was coming for the afternoon. He'd promised Kendra because she was having lunch with the girls, including Stella. He prayed Stella would keep her mouth shut.

He would wait to eat with Connor. Just then, his mobile rang.

"Marcus, here."

"Hey, Marcus, Carey Stevenson here. Last night, Stella mentioned you might have some cars for us to auction at the ball. I'm ringing to work out logistics. Can I arrange for someone to collect the cars?"

Last night? Stella went out last night? Did she meet this guy? And was it work or a date?

He'd been trying to play it cool having her in his home. He'd never lived with a woman since leaving home and having Stella in his house confused him. He loved having her here, and he'd swear he would have hated it.

"Can you ring Tom at Bad Boys? He'll have the details."

"Great. Stella tells me you're under the weather."

Did she now? "I'm fine."

"So, we'll see you at the ball?"

We'll? Was he taking Stella? "I'm not sure. I may be out of town." Liar… But he wouldn't attend if Stella was going with Carey. He couldn't bear watching them all evening. *Then you take her, idiot.*

"That's a shame. It never hurts to have a racing car driver there when the cars go up for auction." When he said nothing, Carey said, "Catch you soon, bye."

If he wasn't so riled up with jealousy, he'd laugh. For the first time in his life he understood the emotions of wanting a woman for more than a fling. He should have seen this coming. He'd always known Stella was different. At first he'd thought it was because they were two of a kind who never got too deeply involved with anyone. Protect yourself.

How was it that Stella was braver than him? A man who sped round a track at over one-hundred-fifty miles per hour with little fear in his head.

Marcus took an ice-cold Coke onto the balcony and looked out over the sea. Did he love Stella? This possessiveness and need to have her around all the time, was it because it scared him to be on his own, knowing what was to come? Or was it genuine?

He loved hearing her laughter, hearing her sing in the shower and having real food to eat, but most of all, he loved that he had someone to talk to, someone who could understand what he was going through and not judge or pepper him with opinions. Oh, he knew what she wanted him to do, to have the operation, but she'd said it once and not mentioned it again.

The only miserable thing about having her in his home was she wasn't in his bed. Not that he'd been able to do much loving until now. It was amazing how his cock understood when he was feeling better.

The doorbell rang, and he heard the door open, and an excited Connor came running.

"Look, Uncle Marcus. Look what daddy bought me."

In the past he would have been able to pick up the little boy and swing him round, but not at the moment.

"Hey, kiddo. They look like golf clubs." A little plastic set. He looked up at Tom as he came out onto the balcony, too.

"All right, Connor. I told you about Uncle Marcus's back and he might not play with you today." Tom raised an eyebrow, asking if he was okay. "Sorry about letting ourselves in, but Kendra gave me a key for emergencies and I thought…"

Tom knew how bad his back was and was fighting him on not letting Kendra know.

"I'm good today. How about I set up a little golf course around the house for you, Con?"

"Will you?" Connor grabbed his hand to lead him inside.

"Connor, wait until Marcus is ready and remember to be good. Uncle Marcus has a very sore back and you know how awful it was when you got sick."

"He doesn't look sick."

"Remember when mommy was sick, we couldn't see it either."

Connor's smile disappeared, and he hugged Marcus around his legs. "Mommy loved hugs when she was sick. It made her feel better and you don't have anyone to hug you."

Marcus's heart somersaulted. It was such a simple gesture, and the kid was right. Sort of. He had Stella—for now. Maybe he should enjoy this while he had the chance.

"Thanks, buddy."

"I'll leave you two to play for the afternoon. Kendra will pick him up in a couple of hours. Hey, I got a call from Carey and the cars are organized. It was a nice thing you did getting a Porsche from Damian."

"I did nothing but ask. All I had to do was pick up the phone."

"Still, Stella is ecstatic. She has a fantastic list of auction items now and I suspect she'll make loads of money for this charity." He bent to hug his son. "You be good."

"Love ya' Daddy."

"Right back at you, kiddo." Tom kissed his head before he left.

Marcus looked down at Connor's little face. A lump formed in his throat. God, he loved this kid. For the first time, he wondered what it would be like to have a son of his own. A child who loved him unconditionally and who he'd protect with his last breath. Someone he was responsible for. That was a frightening thought. He'd do a bloody better job than his father did. Then again, he had some sympathy for his father having to deal with Kendra's leukemia. He didn't know what he'd do if anything were to happen to Connor and he was only the uncle. How did Tom do this every day? He'd struggle to let his son out of his sight.

"Hungry?"

Connor followed him inside and put his clubs on the floor near the lounge. "Depends."

Marcus laughed. Clever kid. "How does Stella's mac and cheese sound? And then perhaps a round of 'find the sinks' golf followed by ice cream."

"What's 'find the sinks' golf?"

He winked. "You have to count the number of shots you take to get a rolled-up sock into every sink in the house. If you beat my record you win ten bucks."

"Ten dollars? That sounds like a lot of fun. Can we play now?"

"Before lunch? What if it takes all afternoon?"

Connor's little face screwed up as he concentrated on that quandary. "I guess food would be good first. Mommy might get here before I eat and I love Aunt Stella's mac and cheese."

"That's my favorite boy."

"You're so lucky having Aunt Stella staying with you. She's a much better cook than Mommy. Are you in love with Aunt Stella? Is that why she lives here? Daddy moved in with Mommy because they were in love." He clambered onto the stool by the kitchen bench. "I'd love it if you married Aunt Stella."

Marcus laughed, but emotions bombarded him as Connor's words sunk in. He could do a lot worse. "She's here because she's looking after me while I'm sick. It's no fun being sick on your own." That was so true.

"But if you married her you'd always have someone to look after you when you're sick. I think you love her. Everyone loves Stella."

"She might not love me."

Connor's smile dimmed. "Mommy says you have no trouble getting girls. I heard her tell Daddy. So why can't you get Stella to love you?"

"It's not that easy, bud."

"I suppose. Look how long it took my daddy to marry my mommy."

He placed a bowl of heated food in front of his nephew. "Eat up and I'll get the socks and then set the course up."

Out of the mouth of babes... He wished his life was different. He paused as he opened his sock draw. Did he? Did he, really? Well, he sure as hell would like to go back and not crash his car into the wall at over one hundred miles per hour.

CHAPTER ELEVEN

Stella let herself into the apartment, and the first thing that hit her was a sock. A sock tightly rolled up into a ball was really quite hard when it hit her chest. "Wow, that hurt."

Kendra pushed past her and entered the apartment. "Connor Lorde, what are you doing?"

Connor came running. "I'm sorry Aunt Stella, but I'm going for the record."

She looked over Connor's head at Marcus, who was trying not to laugh. "Record?"

"In sink golf. Marcus says I have a chance of posting the top score. I'll when ten dollars."

Kendra looked at Marcus. "Why?" She sighed. "Now he's going to want to do this at home."

"Good shot, buddy. I'm sure if Stella hadn't stepped into the room it would have gone skating into the kitchen for your winning shot."

"Can I try again, please?"

"No. We have to go home."

"Come on, sis, let the little man try again. We Blacks aren't quitters."

"He's a Lorde," Kendra hissed. "And don't go filling his head with win at all costs shi-stuff."

"Please, mommy."

Stella hated to get in the middle of a family argument, but she wanted Connor to win. She knew damn well that there was no record to beat. Marcus was letting the boy think he held a record like Marcus did. "Come on, Kendra. I want your opinion on my dress for the ball, anyway."

"Thanks, Aunt Stella."

The smile Marcus threw her way melted her heart. He loved this boy. Why on earth would he be a terrible father? What made him think that? He wasn't pressuring Connor to be the best; he was simply letting the little boy play a game. He was nothing like his father.

"Kendra, come on."

Once in her room, they could hear Marcus giving Connor instructions for the shot.

Kendra plonked her butt on the end of the bed. "I know I over-reacted, but I saw what my father's pushing to be the best, that Black competitive streak, did to Marcus and I won't let my son be consumed by it. It takes away a child's life to be the best in the world. I don't want that for my son."

She didn't disagree. She could remember as a teen visiting the Black house to see Kendra, and Marcus's father would have him in the yard doing press-ups or other weights. Marcus never had fun. Maybe that's why when he got out from under his father's thumb, and when he hit the racing circuit, he overcompensated. He had freedom, and he'd never had that before. Maybe that's why he became such a womanizer. She wondered if he'd still been a virgin since his father kept him under such lock and key.

"You're worrying for nothing. Connor's too much like his

daddy. Tom, is more laid back and Connor is too. I don't think you have to worry. Besides, you and Tom will make sure he never gets too obsessed with winning."

"I just want him to enjoy life. Life can be short. I don't want him to miss a minute of being a kid."

She moved to sit beside her friend and gave Kendra a hug. "Like you did, you mean?" Kendra had spent most of her teens in hospital battling leukemia. "Please tell me you're not worrying every day about Connor's health?"

"I try not to, but it's hard. Every bruise. Every little sniffle I think is this it?" She burst out crying.

"Oh, honey. I know it's hard but there are no guarantees in life and if you keep on this racing track, you'll end up at the end of your life having missed the joy in it." She handed Kendra a tissue. "Have you talked to anyone about this?"

"Tom. He said virtually the same thing, except he added he was there to hold my hand the whole way through."

"You've got a good man there. Do you know how lucky you are?"

"That's what worries me. I was lucky, twice. What if my luck runs out?"

She hugged her tighter. "I didn't realize luck ran out. Anyway, Marcus wasn't pushing Connor to be the best. There is no score to beat. Who else would Marcus have played this 'sink golf' with? Whatever score Connor achieves will be the best. Think about it. It's just a game."

"I know. I'm sorry for getting weepy, it's just…"

She jumped to her feet. "Oh, my God. You 're pregnant again. That's fantastic!" Joy surged through her along with a small dose of the envy green.

"Sssh, no one is supposed to know yet. I'm not quite three months. I wondered why you didn't pick up I wasn't drinking at lunch."

"I have a lot on my mind at the moment."

"The charity ball? Do you need me to help?" Thank God Kendra didn't realize it was her brother on her mind—all the time.

She moved to her wardrobe to reveal her dress. It wasn't the ball she was worried about. It was Marcus, but she couldn't tell Kendra that. She'd promised Marcus not to reveal his condition, but she was torn. Kendra was her best friend. This wouldn't end well. She'd blame her for not telling her sooner.

"Thanks, but I've virtually finished my piece and Carey is the principal organizer this year."

"I hope Catherine hasn't fallen for him. I thought being older she'd have more sense."

Stella laughed. "Love and common sense is an oxymoron." She swung around with the dress in her arms, and Kendra gasped.

"It's so beautiful. Try it on. I have to see it on."

If trying it on changed the subject, she would do it. The dress was an Oscar De La Renta vintage silk gown in a pale ice blue. It hung low at the front in folds, while tiny straps criss-crossed her back, making a bra unwearable, but then she rarely had to wear a bra, not blessed in the chest department. The satin silk clung to her body, molding to her hips and falling into the most beautiful fish-tale.

She walked across the room as if she were on a catwalk. "It feels gorgeous to wear."

"It reminds me of that stunning yellow dress in How To Lose A Guy in Ten Days, with Kate Hudson. The ice blue on you is amazing with your fair hair and tan."

"I thought the pale blue was more understated."

"It is, but damn girl, you look amazing in this. You're sure to get laid the night of the ball if you go in this. Who are you taking?"

"She's taking me."

Marcus was in the doorway with Connor by his side, and the

heat in his eyes almost made her blush. His possessive tone was plain to all.

And of course, Kendra picked up on the tension in the air. "Is there something I should know about going on here?"

"Marcus is going to marry Aunt Stella."

Kendra almost fell off the bed. "What?"

"I'm not."

More's the pity, Stella thought.

Marcus said, "Hey, bud. We talked about this."

Connor put his hands on his hips and faced his uncle. "Uncle Kade said some man will snap her up before Uncle Marcus wakes up and sees what's in front of him. I'm awake and I see her. So, I'll marry her. I don't want a stranger to snap her up, whatever that means, but it doesn't sound good."

"Have you been eavesdropping again, my boy," his mother scolded.

"I can't help it. Sometimes adults forget I'm there."

Marcus cleared his throat. "I think you're a little young for Stella."

Connor's face scrunched up and his eyes filled with tears. "Don't let her be snapped. I don't want Aunt Stella hurt."

Marcus bent and gathered the boy in his arms, and Stella noticed the wince of pain. He shouldn't be doing this and she stepped towards him, but he bent and whispered something in Connor's ear, and the boy's smile was back.

"Okay. I promise," was all the little boy said.

Kendra looked at her watch. "Gosh, I'm late. Come on, Connor. Say thank you to Marcus and Stella, and go get your clubs." When he left the room, she turned on Stella. "You and I are going to have a long talk." To her brother she added, "And keep it in your pants. If you hurt Stella, I'll... I'lll... grrr I don't know what I'll do, but I'll be really mad."

Marcus kissed Kendra's cheek as she slipped past to follow her son. Then he turned to look at her.

"Don't take it off."

"I can't wear this round the house."

"If I had my way, while you're staying here, I'd never let you take if off unless I peeled it from your body myself." With that he was gone, leaving her standing there with her heart in her throat, beating so fast she didn't know if she could breathe.

Why? Why did he have to say something like that, just as she'd fortified herself to being kept in the friend zone. His back must be feeling better. That was a mean thing to think, but hell, in front of Kendra, too.

She quickly changed into sweats. She wanted a swim in the pool and then an early night, but they needed groceries. She heard the front door close and went to find Marcus. "I'm going to get groceries. Do you need anything?"

"I'll go with you."

"Are you sure your back's up to sitting in the car?"

"It's time I found out. I'm going spare in the apartment. I need to get out. We could grab a quick dinner at Marlo's."

She looked down at her sweats. "In these?"

"Okay, let's grab something at the supermarket. I'll cook for a change."

All the way to the supermarket, she worried about him squeezed into her little VW, but when he got out he didn't seem to wince at all.

He picked a cart, and they walked around the store like all the other couples there. It was fun pretending. The women gave off envious stares, and she simply smiled like a cat drowning in cream. She pulled out her list but soon realized Marcus didn't do lists.

She reached in and pulled out a jar. "Why? Why would you buy Greg's Hemp Salad Topping?"

"It says hemp and with my back…"

She put it back on the self. "You'll never use it and it won't help your back." Under her breath she added, "Only one thing will really help your back."

"My back is feeling good from the rest."

"Really?" Was he really feeling better? "Can you get me a packet of pasta from the bottom shelf?"

To her surprise, he bent and picked it up with no wince. Yet she was sure she saw one when he picked up Connor. "See? It's much better."

"Do you still need the pills?"

"The nerves are still pinching, so yes, but I'm not in unbearable pain when moving."

Should she leave his house then? If Marcus was almost back to normal... Is that why he was cooking dinner? A thank you and a 'maybe it's time you left'.

"Can we get those pizza bases you can keep in the freezer?"

She sighed. "I've awoken a monster. You can't live on pizza alone."

"True. Wait till you see what I'm cooking you for dinner."

"What's for dessert?" Gosh, she hadn't meant for it to come out so flirtatious, because Marcus's wiggling eyebrows told her that's how he took it.

He moved in close and whispered in her ear, "I'm open to any request. A. N. Y."

Excitement raced across her skin and through her body. Roaming his body with her tongue would make for a tasty dessert. He was feeling better. Good she...

Instead, she said, "I'll find something as we shop."

He just laughed. "I can read you like a road map. I'm sure—"

"Hello, Marcus."

They both looked up, startled at the voice. "Mother." Awkward silence made the temperature drop ten degrees.

"Fancy seeing you in the Supermarket. And is that Stella with you?" The look on her face spoke volumes.

"Hello, Mrs. Black. You're looking well." What else could she say? She'd not stepped foot in the Black house since they threw Kendra out when she became pregnant with Connor. What mother could do that to their child? But they had spoken briefly at Kendra's wedding. Marcus agreed with her, Kendra forgave far too easily. They should never have been invited.

Susan Black was a sparrow of a woman and when she married a domineering man like Alexander Black, her fate was sealed.

Marcus took Stella's elbow. "We must get on. We're in a bit of a hurry."

His mother stepped in his path. "Your father's not well. He wouldn't let me ring you, but he's in hospital."

His fingers dug into her arm where he held her. Obviously, anger within still burned bright for his father. "And I should care why?"

His mother's head tipped forward and Stella couldn't help feeling sorry for her. "Which hospital, Mrs. Black," she asked.

"Cedar."

His mother pleaded. "I know he's a difficult man"—

"This is not the place for this conversation," Marcus said, but more softly. His mother looked so defeated. "I'm not promising anything, but I'll try to see him. Does Kendra know?"

"I rang her from the hospital just before I left to get groceries. She's visiting him tonight."

She watched Marcus's mouth firm. Stella reached for Marcus's hand. "Thank you for letting me know, Mother." He pressed a kiss to her cheek, which surprised her.

"Thank you, my son. I'll let you get on." Before anything else could be said, she walked off.

"Are you all right?" She asked as Marcus stood looking after his mother.

"I could never understand why she stayed with him."

She wanted to hug him. He looked like a hurt little boy who'd just lost his parents. In a way, he had lost them. Neither of them were really there for either Kendra or Marcus, because Mr. Black's children wouldn't be bullied or forced into lives his father tried to dictate. They were both strong. How ironic they'd inherited this strength from their father.

"Some women are not strong enough to be on their own. They put up with such a lot of shit. Look at my mother. She marries the first man to come along after every divorce just so she's not on her own." She looked at Mrs. Black's retreating back and tried to understand how the woman could live with a man whose heart was made of ice. "I swore I'd never end up like my mother. I choose who I'm with and when or if I leave. I will never be dependent on any man."

Marcus shook his head as they continued down the supermarket aisle. "And yet you want to marry?"

"Only if I find—"

"Mr. Right."

"If I don't then I'm content on my own."

"What, no children?" Marcus's question was serious. He wasn't mocking her.

"I can always have a child. I don't need a husband for that."

He suddenly reached out and cupped her cheek. "You'd make a wonderful mother. I hope you get your wish."

I would if it was with you. "At least we both know we'd be much better at parenting than our parents."

Cool as a cucumber as he reached for a bag of crisps he casually said, "I don't plan on having children."

Please don't let that be true. "The way you played with Connor, made me think you'd love a son of your own. I can just imagine a little Marcus junior. If he has your eyes, he'd soon have everyone wrapped around his little finger."

CHAPTER TWELVE

S hit, his head was a mess. He was being pulled in so many directions because he was so unsure of his future. He goddamn wanted a son or daughter who had his eyes. He wanted what Stella said. Yet, he shouldn't.

The mention of his father reminded him of how horrid his childhood had been, and he was so like his father.

His afternoon with Connor was amazing. He was such a great kid and Marcus loved him—a lot! Stella's words hung in his mind. They would be much better parents than their own because they knew what not to do. *Damn right!* So why did icy fear fill his gut at the idea of raising a child?

Probably because his life was such a mess at the moment with the operation and his long-term prognosis, and then there was his track record with women. There was no way he wanted to be a part-time dad. This split family system never turned out well for the kids. When it came to children, you definitely needed to be sure that the person would be with you forever. Kids from split homes had it so tough. Since he'd be terrible at marriage, he wasn't renown for being a one-woman man, he'd always assumed he'd never have a kid.

"Speaking of kids," he said and threw a box of condoms into the shopping cart.

"Just the one box?" Stella teased. "I thought your back was feeling better?"

Just to spite her, he took another box. He hadn't had sex since Maui, and having the hottest woman in LA living down the hall wasn't slowing his libido. God, when he'd seen her in that dress... Even the presence of Connor and Kendra barely kept his hard on at bay.

She was so beautiful, inside and out. He would miss her when she moved out. Why did she have to move out? Did she want to move out? She still checked his pill intake every day. She was so worried he'd become addicted. The perfect friend. She didn't judge, didn't lecture, just merely monitored him. Friendship was something you didn't take for granted, or fool around with, but he longed for more. When had that longing begun?

He was brave enough to admit he loved having her in his house. Having her down the hall, being with him whenever he wanted, made him think he could become a one-woman man. To his surprise, he'd not missed the parade of women who normally came through his front door. He'd not even thought of another woman in weeks.

In the middle of a supermarket aisle, he felt Stella's presence beside him, and her fragrance filled his soul. Perhaps he could do it... Only if that woman was Stella. His heart expanded in his chest. Was this love?

He flashed her a smile as he reached for the most decadent chocolate mousse in the deli department.

"Chocolate mousse?" Stella shook her head. "Not very imaginative. I expected more."

He pulled her close and put his arm around her shoulders. "Oh, you'll get more. Wait and see." He suddenly had the perfect plan to make this night the perfect night, and he was in the condition to see it through.

He would work to make Stella see he could be her Mr. Right and ensure she gave him a second chance.

HE SENT STELLA TO THE POOL WHILE HE PREPARED DINNER. HE was making Chicken Parmigiana. He'd made this recipe before, but only for himself and it was so good. The whole evening would have an Italian flavor. The most romantic country in the world, right? A pity about the garlic, though, for what he had planned later, so he'd gone with cheese sticks instead of garlic bread. He'd also made her favorite selection of salads.

Everything was going exactly as he'd planned. He'd even changed his sheets and put flowers in his room.

He'd opened a bottle of red to let it breathe. Even though they were having chicken, it would be red because she loved red wine. He'd just finished showering and changing into a pair of black jeans and white t-shirt, when Stella appeared in the living room. She was wearing a dress. Although it wasn't *the* dress of this afternoon, she looked hot enough to combust ice. His gaze longingly followed the hot pink strapless dress to her knees, her tanned legs and down to the strappy sandals she wore.

"Something smells amazing. I'm so hungry."

He couldn't help himself. He walked up to her, cupped her cheeks in his hands and pressed a kiss to those gloss covered lips.

"What was that for?" Her blush made his heart sing. She'd liked it.

"For being you. The best friend a guy could ever have." Her smile dimmed. Shit, he'd said the wrong thing. She didn't want a friend. She wanted a life partner. She was his best friend, but he wanted more to… His back be damned. He would never have the op and learn to live with the pain. Yeah, he was fooling himself, but he wanted it all. He wanted a normal life with a wonderful woman. He wanted to try with Stella. If he couldn't make it work with her he'd never make it work with anyone.

She blinked a few times, and the smile wavered. "I'll always be your friend."

"Oh, honey, I know that. What if I want to be more than friends?" Her mouth dropped open. He rushed on, "Not FWB. I know you're looking for Mr. Right and we both know I'm not Mr. Right material, but I could be. I could be if you give me a chance." He led her into the dining room.

"This is so beautiful," she whispered. "Where, and how, did you find my favorite flowers? They weren't here when I went for a swim."

"Sometimes it pays to be a famous ex-formula one racing car driver." He rang his florist friend, Bob and get him to personally deliver bunches of roses, peonies, and orchids.

"Or a man who buys so many 'kiss off' flowers his florist will do anything for him."

He shrugged. "Guilty as charged, but that is the old Marcus."

"The old Marcus? Am I meeting the new Marcus tonight?"

"Most definitely." He held the chair out for her.

He poured her some sparkling water and also a glass of red wine. A big glass of red wine.

"Hey, are you trying to get me sloshed? I can't drink wine on an empty stomach."

He scoffed. "You can drink men twice your size under the table. Pace yourself. For your first course, I've made a goat's cheese and asparagus mini-tart. Excuse me while I get it ready for you."

The meal couldn't have gone any better. She loved his chicken parmigiana. They had just finished eating when she asked, "Did you ring Kendra about your father?"

He sighed. He didn't want to talk about this father, but if he was changing to Mr. Right, he assumed he had to let her in and if anyone could understand, it was Stella. She'd been a visitor in his home for most of her teenage life.

"I spoke to Kendra. She said mother was exaggerating as usual. Father's had three stents put in but he'll be fine as long as he slows down a bit."

"Are you going to visit him in the hospital?"

He took a sip of wine. "I don't know. What do you think?"

Her eyes widened. He'd scored points here. "Your father's a... difficult man. Lawyers always seem hard to warm to. My father, the movie producer, is simply selfish and cares for no one but himself. Yours on the other hand, he at least thought the things he did were for your benefit. He's always, in his heartless way, cared about you. Mine couldn't care less if he never heard from me again."

He thought on Stella's words. While his father had driven him to the point of exasperation towards becoming a lawyer and taking over the business, and hadn't cared what his son really wanted to do with his life, his father had always done the things he did to make Marcus's life successful. The only problem was his father had almost cost him his racing career by going behind his back on his first Formula One contract negotiation. It was only the savviness of Marcus's actual lawyer and his open and trustworthy approach that it didn't completely fall apart.

He was kidding himself if he thought his father would ever change, which threw cold water on his idea that he, himself, could change and commit.

I'm not my father.

"So, you're saying he meant well and I should be the dutiful son?"

"I'm saying it's your decision. I can't forgive him for what he did to Kendra. I can't forget those three years of scraping by, trying to raise her son, alone. You were so good to her." She reached across and took his hand. "I've never really thanked you for all you did for my best friend."

"She's my sister and I'd never let anyone hurt her. At one stage I thought I might lose her to cancer. It made me more determined to live my life my way. She gave me the courage to push back at my father and follow my dreams of racing. I love her for that and so much more. She's so strong. Dad underestimated her."

"Then why do you think you'd make a terrible father?"

He had to give an honest answer if this relationship with Stella was ever going to work. "The one thing I value so much in this relationship—I mean, with you and me—is that you know the real me. You already know I'm a selfish jackass, that I'm single minded. You know I'm as busy as fuck because I'm driven to be the best at whatever I do or set out to achieve. Yet, you still enjoy spending time with me."

"Some of those qualities can be good. The selfish one I take umbrage at. You're one of the most generous men I know, and not just with your money. I know you set up the go-kart racing for under privilege kids and that every Sunday afternoon, except when your back's stuffed, you go there and help out."

Don't put me on a pedestal, you'll be disappointed. Hadn't she told him that?

She sat back in her chair and sipped her wine. "Those things don't necessarily make you a terrible father. So, spill. What's up with this no children shit?"

"What if I can't do the long-term thing?" Should he be telling her this when he wanted to see if he could... with her? "I see kids that are shoved between homes, having to deal with blended families, fights over holiday access, maybe switching schools and don't get me started about one parent moving interstate. I don't want that for any child of mine."

Stella's smile faded. "Oh, my God, because you don't think

you'll be the 'best' at marriage, you're not even going to try? You're afraid of failure."

He sat up in his chair, his heart pounding faster than an electric drill. Failure? Was that why he never wanted to commit? He swallowed a 'don't be ridiculous' reply because she might be right.

"You do know it's acceptable not to be the best at everything?"

I thought she knew me? He had to be the best. Didn't he? He ran a hand through his hair. "But you have to be the best for your child."

She rose and moved to crouch by his chair. She took his hands in hers. "The only thing that you really have to be the best at with your child is loving them, and letting them know how much you love them every day. Ensure they're safe and cared for. You would never, ever fail at that no matter if you were a part-time dad, their only parent, or in a committed relationship."

"I would love any child of mine, unreservedly, no matter what they wanted out of their life."

"Like I said, you're very different from your father, and the other thing you must remember is that you wouldn't be doing it alone. You once told me it took a team to make you a formula one winner. Well parenting takes a team too. Look at Kendra. She was a solo mum for a while, but she had you and me. You'd always have Kendra and Tom and the team at Bad Boys. Plus, if you were in a committed partnership, you'd have someone there to support you too."

She made it sound so simple. All he had to do was trust in himself to know he wouldn't fail. He'd always backed himself in anything he took on. When he looked where Stella's petite hands held his, a light bulb lit up his head. She would never let him fail if their relationship didn't work out because that is who she was, a nurturer. She'd always be his friend. What did he have to risk?

He pulled her onto his lap. He pushed a strand of her hair behind her ear. "How did I get so lucky to find a woman like you?"

Then he kissed her. He kissed her how he'd wanted to kiss her from the day she'd moved in, with no holding back. A tiny sliver of fear hit him. He wasn't a coward and he'd worry about his operation later. Hell, with Stella's help he could put it off for years.

He broke the kiss. "This is where, in the movies, I pick you up and carry you into my bedroom but…"

"Just as well I didn't get legless or this beautiful moment might have been ruined."

That's what he loved about Stella, her humor. Despite his condition, she didn't hold back. Perhaps that's why he'd never grown bored with her, in bed or out. He was so very far from feeling bored.

As soon as they entered his bedroom, Stella turned to him with eyes shining brightly. "Orchids. You know how much I adore them." He'd filled every vase he had in the house and put them around the room. She stood before him and said, "You wanted this to be a special night. Are we really going to try this?"

"I want to try so badly. You'll need to help me as I'm bound to make mistakes. I've never done this before."

"Neither have I, but it's exciting. We can learn together. We won't hide our relationship from anyone anymore?"

He nodded. "We can tell Kendra and Tom tomorrow. Let's ring them in the morning, and go to their house for lunch."

His heart took flight at her answering smile. She stood back and unzipped her dress, stepping out of it as it fell to the floor. His breath caught. She was the hottest thing he'd ever seen.

She stood before him naked except for a tiny thong and her

strappy sandals. His hard cock grew even bigger. The sight of her small breasts, with their hardened nipples, made his mouth water. Even though he already knew every curve of her delicious body, this felt different, felt new.

As he reached to pull his T-shirt over his head, he felt her fingers at the buttons of his jeans. He loved her gasp as she found he'd gone commando. They faced each other, completely naked. There'd been much touching and kissing along the way, and he was standing fully to attention.

"Lie down," she ordered, and he had to admit with his back, it probably was the best position, but he hated giving up the control. He did as she asked, and as she rose over him, perhaps he wasn't so upset at losing control.

She reached to the sideboard for the box of condoms they'd bought in the supermarket and tore it open. It was torture, as she used her hands and mouth to sleeve him. His eyes rolled back in his head as she slowly sank down. She was heaven and this might be over too quickly if he wasn't careful.

He let her slow ride him, and gritted his teeth against the desire to move beneath her. He smoothed her back with the heels of his hands, stroked those long legs gripping his sides. He loved how her back arched as passion took her, adored her uninhibited enjoyment. She was as fearless of their physical passion as she was of wearing her heart on her sleeve and his heart swelled within his chest, wanting to give this woman everything. She whispered his name again and again, her rhythm driving him towards completion far too soon. He cupped her breasts, teasing each stiffened nipple with his fingers, dying inside as she rocked and twisted, knowing how to squeeze and tease him. He couldn't think, but couldn't thrust up, it was torture. Instead, he took her hips in a tight grip, and urged her to move faster and harder, but she enjoyed taunting him and wasn't about to relinquish control.

She leaned down so her pert breasts rubbed his chest and

whispered, "Not yet. Only when I say... I want to come with you."

The slow slide up and down was torture and pleasure.

"Oh, God, Marcus, that feels so good."

Her husky voice led him closer and closer to the edge. "I'm almost there," he groaned. In a heartbeat and after a slide down his hard length, he went under, submerged in hot, all-consuming flames of ecstasy. Over and over, ripples of pleasure blanketed his mind and body. It took some time before he realized the long groan of fulfillment filling his bedroom was his.

As he tried to open his eyes, Stella collapsed on his chest, her body shaking with her release. He pulled her close, and they continued to tremble together, thankful she'd come the second after he had. They lay tightly entwined riding the waves to ripples as the pleasure slowed and their heartbeats returned to normal.

He wanted more. He wanted to hear her scream his name again and again.

"On your knees, and come here. Hold on to the headboard."

He positioned her over his face and gave her little time to recover from her orgasm before his tongue and mouth set about making her scream until her voice grew hoarse and her legs shook. He teased with his lips and tongue, eating her hot, wet sweetness, and couldn't get enough. He never wanted it to end, with his name on her lips marking her his.

She threw her head back, screamed his name, shuddering as she came. Her knuckles whitened where they gripped the wood. He loved her ability to slide from one orgasm to the next. He loved hearing his name and knowing they'd agreed to go on this new journey together.

Finally, he took mercy and slowly brought her down from the pinnacle of pleasure. She stretched out beside him, her body so sensitive she moaned at a simple caress.

"Wait until I have my strength back. I'll return the favor with fervor," she whispered as she stroked his cheek. "As long as your back isn't giving you pain."

He kissed her hand. "Look what those words have done to me. The only pain I'm in is of wanting you again."

He was hard as a rock. She smiled and moved over him. At the first touch of her tongue on his cock, he knew her words to work him into a fervor would come true. As she took him deep with her mouth, the world blanked and all that mattered was Stella.

His Stella.

CHAPTER THIRTEEN

"I knew there was more to the house being painted. The way Marcus acted when he saw you in that ball dress; possessive is too passive a word. So, when did this all begin? At Lexie and Kade's wedding in Maui?" Kendra asked as they sat around the table, eating the lunch they'd picked up. Connor had wanted sushi, so they'd visited the fish market, walking hand in hand for the first time, and Stella wondered if her feet even hit the ground.

They were a couple. She knew it was early days, but she had a fantastic feeling about everything.

She looked at Marcus. "Sort of?"

"What the hell does that mean?" Kendra persisted.

Marcus spoke up. "We've been friends with benefits since your twentieth birthday at Porter's Bar, but in Maui we discovered we wanted more."

Hearing him say those words... it still seemed unreal. He was committing to a relationship.

"Since my... all these years?" She turned to look at Stella. "You kept this from me?"

"Until today there was nothing I was proud of sharing."

That shut her friend up.

"I, for one, think it's wonderful. I'm happy for Marcus and Stella. Two people I despaired of ever settling down found each other. They should write stories about this sort of thing." Stella had always liked Tom, but she could jump up and hug him.

She watched Marcus closely, but he didn't flinch at the words 'settling down'. "So, are you going to live with Marcus once they've finished painting your apartment? Surely it's done by now?" Nor did he flinch at Kendra asking if they would remain living together.

She hadn't thought about that. She'd just been happy to finally have a relationship that wasn't hidden from those they knew. Stella wanted to stay in Marcus's apartment because she still worried about his back and the pain meds he was on. She knew how strong his will power was when he put his mind to something, but even so… if his pain grew worse or he had another episode like in Maui what would he do? Those pills were addictive, and he had enough problems with just his back. Living together might be too much straight away and she didn't want to spook him before they'd even really started.

She didn't know what to say because Marcus forbade her from telling Kendra or Tom about how painful his back was. The painting ruse wouldn't hold for long.

"We haven't thought that far ahead but the paint fumes are still quite strong, so I guess I'll have the pleasure of having Stella with me for at least another week, or maybe until after the charity ball in two weeks. It seems silly to move your belongings and work home when you're busy with last-minute tasks."

Her body warmed. Marcus still wanted her with him.

"That sounds sensible," Tom said. "Speaking of the ball, I assume you're going with each other?"

"Of course." She smiled at Marcus's response. Her intention had always been to attend the ball with Marcus, but now it would be as his girlfriend.

Just then they heard little Matti cry. "She's woken up at last."
Marcus rose. "I'll get her," he said and left the room.
"I'll come too. She'll probably need changing." Tom followed behind.

"Me too," said six-year-old Connor, and all the males in the family left the room.

As soon as they were alone, Kendra said, "Don't hurt him, Stella. This is the first time I've seen him look at all interested in a relationship. And I know you like to play the"—

"I love him." There, she'd said it. "I called off our FWB in Maui because I wanted more. I thought he'd be pleased our arrangement had ended but... He said he wants to have a relationship and I'm thrilled."

Kendra chewed her bottom lip. "Maybe it's you I have to worry about getting hurt. He's never done this before. Does he love you?"

Her smile dimmed. "He says so. He definitely has feelings for me, powerful feelings, but love? He's only seeing how this goes. Please don't tell him how I feel. It might frighten him off. I'm going to have to take this slowly."

"Very slowly," her friend said. "Do you think it's a good idea to continue living at his house?"

"I don't know." That was the truth. She didn't know. All she knew was it was probably wise at the moment. Someone had to ensure he didn't overuse his meds.

"Whatever happens, promise me it won't affect our friendship. You're the closest thing to a sister I have, and I love you both. I don't want to have to take sides. He is my brother, my big brother who stood by me through cancer and being a single mum."

She rose and hugged Kendra, then went to look out across the beautiful backyard. It was a family place with a small cycle on the wooden deck, a swing hanging from a tree and the swimming pool full of colorful inflatable animals. She wanted this so much. Did Marcus? She took hope from the fact that once Marcus committed to something, he always gave it one hundred percent. "I'm going into this with my eyes wide open. I'm trying not to get my hopes up. It's hard getting things right the first time so… The chances of us making it aren't great, but I have to try. I don't want to live with 'what if?'."

"Tom and I will do anything to help."

She turned to face Kendra. "I don't think there is anything anyone can do. We have to navigate this on our own and I'm as scared as hell."

Kendra rose and came to stand beside her. "It scared me when Tom came back into my life. Thank God, I gave him a chance. Unless you try, you'll never know if it's meant to be."

Before she could reply, the men and Connor arrived back. Marcus carried a giggling, drooling Matti in his arms. Hormones and ovaries started quivering. Oh, to have Marcus's child and hold them in her arms. She'd risk anything for a chance to do that and have the life she dreamed of with the man she'd fallen in love with.

"This little girl wants a swim," Marcus announced. Matti clapped her hands and giggled.

"Marcus says you brought your swimsuits so let's head outdoors and let the kids play in the pool."

She nodded her head at Tom's suggestion. "I'll go get changed. I could do with a swim too." She needed it to cool off her overheated imagination and her bouncing ovaries.

"You look happy."

Marcus briefly took his gaze off the little girl he was holding up in the pool. Her water wings splashing him as she flapped her arms and kicked her little legs. "Are you saying I don't normally?"

Tom laughed. "Well, you seem happier then normal. More relaxed. I think I like Stella's influence on you."

"She's pretty special." And she looked so hot lying on the lounger in a swimsuit that left little to the imagination. She was in great shape. He wondered what their children would look like. He'd love a little girl with the same dancing eyes and wicked smile as hers.

Tom noticed him staring. "You've got it bad, bro'. It's about time. I thought you'd never get over your fear."

He didn't deny it. "Not fear exactly. More like self-preservation." He moved, pulling Matti through the water. At twenty-months old loved the water and would stay in the pool all day if she could. Her delighted squeals filled the yard. "She's going to be a handful when she reaches sixteen."

"*Sixteen?* She's a handful now. Do you think you'd ever want a child of your own? They change your life, but it's fantastic; scary, thrilling, emotional, unconditional love. There is nothing like it in the world."

He looked down at Matti's smiling face, so full of trust that Marcus would keep her safe. He loved his niece and yes, he was scared at the idea of being responsible for a child, but the love that filled his heart at the idea of his own child showed he wanted children. Before he could reply, Connor came running.

"Watch, Daddy," and Connor bombed them, causing waves to crash over Matti's head and she coughed and spluttered and then burst into tears.

Kendra sat up. "Connor Lorde, you get out of that pool. What have I said about scaring Matti?"

"Sorry, mommy."

"You apologize to your sister."

He swam across and kissed the still screaming Matti on her cheek.

Marcus lifted her above his head and blew kisses on her little tummy, and soon she was laughing again. "All better?" he asked the little girl. Kendra arrived and lifted her from Marcus's arms. "She probably needs a potty break, anyway. Connor, you can get out too. Five minutes in the sin bin for breaking the rules."

"Oh, please mommy?"

"Do as you're told, kiddo. Five minutes," said Tom.

Marcus didn't understand how they could be so strong. One look at Connor's face and he would have given in.

"You'll learn. Give in and you make a rod for your back, but boy it's tough." Tom exited the pool, too.

He turned to Tom. "While I'm here, I think I'll swim a few lengths to stretch out my back."

"How is the back? Will you be back in the office soon, or continuing to work from home? I bet having Stella living with you is an added incentive to stay home, but don't forget you have Carlos's Porsche to test with him, just before the ball, and then we have that trip scheduled to Miami."

"I'll come into the office tomorrow, but maybe not stay all day."

"Fine. We can go over the Miami information and decide what our offer might be. I also think we need to start the discussion with Sully about stepping up. If you go to Miami, I'll need him to be my second in charge. I think the share package offer we worked out is fair."

Shit. He'd forgotten about Carlos. Carlos brought a lot of business their way. The team was currently customizing a Porsche Carrera for him and he expected Marcus to test drive it. His back was better than it had been before Maui, because Stella ensured he followed the doctor's routine religiously. He was also holding his own in the making-love department, which was really important to a woman like Stella. She was the female equivalent of him. She loved sex and was a sensual being who wasn't ashamed of her body or the giving and receiving of pleasure. It's probably what kept them together for so long in the beginning.

His inner demon pushed away the guilt. He wasn't being truthful with her. Sex would always be one of the most important aspects of their relationship. It was important that libidos matched, but his back surgery could put paid to that, and he couldn't bring himself to tell her. He would have to tell her and soon. How could he let her think they could have this perfect life, a family, when he could become impotent? Doctor Forrester had advised him to bank his sperm prior to the operation.

Tom noted his silence. "You have told Stella about Miami?"

"Of course." That wasn't a lie. He had told her about Miami, just not that he would definitely run it. She had probably guessed, though.

"And she's happy to live there for a few years?"

"We've only just started this relationship. There's still a lot to sort out."

Tom stopped toweling off. "You want her to go with you? You're not starting this relationship because you know you have a way out by moving?"

"Of course I want her to come with me." He did. He really did. But what if she didn't want to go?

"You have asked her, you know, told her you're going to be heading up the Miami office for a couple of years?"

"I've told her it will probably be me running it. I just haven't told her it's confirmed."

Tom shook his head. "Shit. You best tell her before she finds out from someone else, like Kendra or even Lexie, when she gets back next week."

"I will." With that, he pushed off and dived under the water. *Failure.* Every muscle seemed tight, and tension filled his joints. He hated failure and already he was on the back foot with this relationship stuff. How did guys do this? Open up and be truthful when it meant they could lose everything?

His gut clenched the further he swam, thinking that on day one he'd already fucked up.

A splash interrupted his musing, and a body cut through the water next to him. Stella popped up beside him and wrapped her arms around his neck.

"Kendra and Tom have taken the kids inside for a sleep. The water looked more inviting because you're in it. I couldn't resist." She wrapped her legs around his waist and kissed him.

Blood fled south, and he forgot what might go wrong and focused on what was so right. When she was in his arms, her body pressed to his, nothing else touched them.

She rubbed against his straining erection. "I think it's time we went home and had a rest, too. What do you think?"

"I think it's going to take a while for this hard on to go down if you keep doing that."

She laughed and broke free of him, swimming to the side of the pool and pulling herself up on the tiles. "This is where we women have the upper hand. I can walk inside and no one knows how wet and aching I am for you," she said huskily.

"That image is not helping, you vixen."

She stood up and shook herself before grabbing a towel and sensually rubbing it across her breasts and between her legs.

"You said you wanted to go home? Keep that up and I'll be in this pool until midnight with balls of blue."

Her laughter followed her inside and his grin wouldn't die, neither would his erection. Would he always want her this much? He hoped so.

He swam a few laps to calm his body. His brain switched to work and the expansion into Miami. What a crap business owner he was, because suddenly Miami didn't sound so exciting. Miami was his idea. He wondered if he went looking for more because of boredom and fear of his back's condition, but now he was with Stella and his life held many possibilities. Did he really want or need Miami and expansion? Why couldn't he be content with what he had? Bad Boy Autos was the best customization garage in LA. Hell, probably in the country. Did he need more branches to prove that? And prove it to whom?

For the first time in his life, he had to consider someone else, and it pleased him to know he didn't mind. That had to be a good sign. He would willingly make changes if he had to for Stella.

CHAPTER FOURTEEN

The next morning Tom delivered a loan car to him. Tom was lending him his vintage Dodge. Marcus couldn't get in and out of his sports cars without putting too much pressure on his back, so he was borrowing a Dodge Dart with wide rather than bucket seats, and getting in and out of the car was easier for his back.

He owned several cars which he kept at Bad Boy Autos, but they were all sports cars, ranging from his Formula One replica to his Aston Martin Vantage F1 Edition. That was his favorite car to drive, but at the moment it was agony on his back.

"I expect to get her back with not a scratch on her."

He gave Tom that look. "I think I know how to drive."

Tom shook his head. "And no speeding tickets."

"Oh, fuck off. But thanks for the loan. It will really help." He could actually drive himself around without being in absolute agony all day.

Just then Stella arrived at the park garage. "What a beautiful car. Thanks, Tom. He won't admit it but those sports cars are out of the question to drive for now. Ready to go?"

"Where are you two off to?" Tom asked.

"We're going to Stella's office to go over the applications for the apprentice mechanic jobs that we'll put forward to go in the draw to win a place at the auction. Do you want to help with the selection?"

"I trust your judgement. Besides, I'm taking Connor toy shopping. He wants to go toy shopping with his pocket money. He's going to be in total shock when he realizes how much things cost, but he has to learn money doesn't grow on trees. You have to work for every penny."

He admired Tom's stance. Looking back on his upbringing, he realized his family had given him the best of everything, yet he didn't remember his childhood as being a particularly happy one. Money and happiness did not walk hand in hand.

Stella placed a kiss on Tom's cheek. "Remind Kendra she's got to confirm the band has everything they need for the ball."

"I will. She's really looking forward to singing her latest hit she's written for James Tan."

"She has such a beautiful voice. I think she sings it better than Tan."

His sister sang like an angel but she gave up the chance at a career in the spotlight for Tom and her family. She continued to write songs for many artists though and was quite successful. He wondered why women were so good at putting family first. Men were more selfish. Or was that only him?

THEY REACHED STELLA'S OFFICE IN UNDER TWENTY MINUTES. SHE worked out of a small building near the OC Museum of Art. She paid for it out of her own money and had a small staff of three: Jacob, Tamra, and Claire.

Tamra greeted them as they arrived. "Hi, Stella, Marcus. I've gone through all the applications. There were over three-hundred. I've grouped them into, probable's, possibles, probably not, and definitely not. Feel free to move applications around into different piles but I wanted to simplify it so you didn't have to spend too much time on this today."

"I'd like to look at all of them," Marcus said. When Stella's eyebrow rose he added, "I want everyone to have a fair chance."

He remembered when he'd first turned up at thirteen to the Go-Kart racing he now donated his money and time to. Ross Chambers, an ex-Indy race car driver, had set it up twenty-years-ago to help troubled kids in Huntington Beach. Marcus had been one of those troubled kids and without Ross's help he'd never have got to Formula One, or been a world champion.

It only took one mentor, one person to change the course of a kid's life.

Stella slipped her hand in his. "I agree. We'll look at all the applications. We have time."

An hour in, and Stella threw an application on the table. "Gosh, this is so difficult. All the ones I've read so far deserve to go in the draw but they're so young. What if being a mechanic is not really for them? We may give it to the wrong person and someone who really wants to be a mechanic misses out." She read out loud. "Simone is in foster care as her parents died of Covid. She scores well in math and physics but loves working with her hands. She's interested in vintage cars, as her father restored cars and she used to help him. She'd love to start an apprenticeship at Bad Boy Autos as she would feel like she was closer to her father and living the life she really wants." Stella's eyes welled with tears. "I want you to give her a job now. If we put these in the draw, she only has a one in three-hundred chance."

She was right. His lips tightened with frustration.

"This young girl would love working at Bad Boy Autos with Lexie there as a mentor."

He wished he could do so much more, but he didn't have enough positions. "I'm happy if all of them go in the draw but what gets me is that I can only offer for three. If I open up more businesses, then I could offer more each year."

"This is important to you, isn't it? It's not merely an idea to contribute to my ball. You want to help these kids."

He stood up to stretch his back. "I keep thinking that if I hadn't met Ross, if he hadn't seen something in me, I don't know where'd I have ended up. Maybe I'd be the stuffy lawyer father wanted."

"One bonus of that would be your back would still be working as it should." She smiled, but he didn't smile back. He couldn't. If he had the same choice again, he'd still pick racing over being a lawyer.

"There are always a lot of 'ifs' in life. If only my father hadn't been a bully. If only I hadn't resented him so much. If only Colter hadn't rammed my car…"

"I remember you always arguing with your father. Screaming matches. He never hit you though."

"There are other forms of abuse that aren't physical. He would tell me that without his help, I'd never amount to anything, that I needed the family name and the family firm. It made me more determined to prove him wrong." It'd turned him to a win at all costs, driven to succeed, selfish man.

"It's horrible how our families affect and shape our lives. I've let my biological clock get very close to running out because my parents' behavior clouded my view of family. I wonder if I'd already be married with loads of children if my parents didn't view marriage as a revolving door." He was bloody glad she wasn't already married because his younger self would have run for the hills if she'd mentioned marriage.

She gave a weak smile. "Now I know what I want—children and family—I won't let myself marry anyone who isn't committed to that goal. I don't want my children brought up in a broken home."

"There are no certainties in life, Stella. My parents stayed together, but they set little example of a great family life either. I could never stay with someone just for the children's sake because they can see through that too. Kendra's embraced family fully, and she looks happy. I think you just have to be ready for the responsibility of family, and ensure it's with the right person." He walked around to peer over her shoulder. "Fate. Sometimes it makes me wonder. One chance meeting changed my life, and if we hadn't started our friends with benefits would we be here now?"

"That's why you give your time and money to Ross Chamber's Go-Kart charity, because you know without him your life would have been different, and probably not in a good way." She hesitated. "Why don't we set up another charity. We could take applications from kids like these and set up a mechanics intern placements charity. These kids could see if they want this kind of job or life. We could go to all the mechanical garages across the country and get them to come to us when they need interns. It'd save them money on recruitment, and if we raise enough money, we could pay for the first year of training should they decide to take on an apprentice." Her enthusiasm built. "With your name behind the charity we could really make a difference."

God, she was an amazing woman. Nothing phased her. She thought that with the right people, you could do anything. She thought of everyone else rather than herself. She wanted to try to do this because she'd read these kids' backgrounds and it affected her. She believed in what she was doing and it was always for other people; people less fortunate than her.

"How do you do this? Always come up with ideas to help others."

"Oh, please. It's easy to help when you have money and time."

"It's not just money. Plenty of people have money and time, but they don't do what you do. You put your heart and soul into every charity you're involved with. You really care about the people you try to help. It's why you're so easy to love."

"Love?"

He helped her to her feet and cupped her face in his hands. "I love you, Stella Perry. The day you propositioned me in Porter's Bar was the best thing that ever happened to me."

"Better than winning the world championship?" she teased, her face flushing with heat.

He hugged her tightly. "That was a fleeting moment in my life. You're for the rest of my life." He meant it. The idea of a life with one woman—with Stella—didn't frighten him. The thought that he might not fulfil her dream of children niggled at the back of his mind and he pushed the fear of disappointing her away. What if he couldn't give her children? Would she still love him? Would she stay with him?

"I love you too, so much. I wish we weren't in my office. I wish I could strip that t-shirt from your hot, desirable body, and show you how much I love you, but we need to give our complete undivided attention to these piles of paper. I think we pick fifty kids who deserve a real chance at these three apprenticeships and do the draw from those, but use the others as the basis of our new intern charity. What shall we name it?"

"How about 'Black Perry Mechanical Internships?'"

She frowned "Sounds like blackberry?"

"Easy to remember? Okay, Black and Perry Mechanical Internships."

"I suppose it has your name in it, which will be really important. Maybe we take a few days to think about it. We'll need a lawyer to draw up the papers. It would be great if we could find one who'd do it pro-bono."

Marcus knew who might do that.

Stella carried on talking. "How about we each put in $50k for startup money?"

"You'd do that for me? How about I raffle off my Aston Martin and use the proceeds to start us off?"

She looked up at him with eyes wide. "You love that car. It's worth about $165k."

"It kills my back, and it's not a family car." Wow, he'd earn points for that.

"Oh, you say the sweetest things," she said and kissed him, her tongue slipping between his lips, stroking the inside of his mouth until his body hardened and he could easily push her up against the wall and take her from behind.

He broke off the kiss and, breathing heavily in her ear, said, "Let's pick our top fifty and then I'll take you home and reward you for your generosity."

She rubbed against his erection, and he groaned. "I like the way you think."

While he wanted to hurry, they took their time and selected fifty kids who they thought were ready to take on an apprenticeship.

LATER THAT NIGHT, AFTER THEY'D HAD A LOVELY AFTERNOON IN bed, Stella was out meeting with her team regarding seating and tables for the ball, and Marcus set off on a mission of his own.

He'd learned his father was now convalescing at home and he was visiting with a mission in mind. His mother seemed to think his father wanted to mend bridges. Father had tried with Kendra, and apologized for the way he'd behaved when she found herself pregnant. She'd refused to name the father of her child and their father had thought throwing her out of home would make her cave and reveal all. He forgot his children were like him. Stubborn and resourceful.

He stood at the door to his family home but couldn't quite

bring himself to simply walk in. So he rang the doorbell. Less than a minute later, his mother answered the door.

"Marcus, how wonderful to see you. Do come in."

He moved inside and kissed his mother on her cheek. "Hi, Mother. I thought I'd pop by and see how father is doing."

"He'll be so pleased to see you. He's in his study. I'll make us all some coffee."

"Isn't he supposed to be resting?"

"You know your father. He always thinks he knows best."

Too true. As he made his way to his father's study, he remembered the times he was ordered there to be scolded for underperforming, or for doing something that wasn't in his father's grand plan. Why did this room make him feel like he was ten years old again?

This time he didn't knock. The door was open anyway. He entered and was shocked to see his father lying on the sofa with his eyes closed. He looked old. He looked tired and strained, and Marcus realized he might not have his father for too much longer and he needed to have his say. He needed to tell him he was a shitty father, but that he'd given him traits that saw him achieve at the highest level. He recognized much of his father within him, but he also knew he would act differently with any child of his own. No pressurizing, simply encouragement and love.

His father's eyes flickered open and, for one second, Marcus saw a look of relief and joy. Then his father pushed himself into a sitting position and the uptight lawyer was back. "Marcus, what a pleasant surprise. Come sit."

He smiled at his father, who had never given him such a warm welcome before. "Hi, Father. I'm pleased to see you looking well."

So formal. He remembered Connor and Tom together and couldn't remember a time his father laughed and joked with him. Marcus eased himself into the leather chair by his father's desk.

His father must have seen because he said, "Kendra tells me your back is bad again. Is it time for more surgery?"

He didn't want to discuss his back. "Dr. Forrester and I are looking at my options." For once, his father didn't badger him for more info.

His father eyed him like he would an opponent in court. "What brings you by?"

He looked his father straight in the eye. "I'd like your help with something."

His father's eyes widened, and he didn't gloat like Marcus expected. He'd swear his father looked humbled. "Well, come on. What do you need my help with?"

"Stella and I want to set up a charity to place kids in internships within other chop shops and garages. We'd like a lawyer on the board; a lawyer whose firm would work pro-bono for the charity."

His father sat up straighter. "You want me? My firm?"

"You're very good at what you do. You have a name for honesty and winning, and I thought it might help heal the wounds in our relationship."

Just then, his mother entered with coffee. "No raised voices, that's a good sign. You mustn't get your father angry in his condition."

Marcus bit back a retort that it was only his father who started arguments. "Actually, I was just asking father for a favor."

"Our son wants me to be on the board of a new charity he's setting up and provide legal services pro bono."

"Your father is stepping back from the day to day running of the firm. He's supposed to be slowing down."

"I'll be bored to death doing nothing. This could be just the thing I need. Tell me more, son."

Marcus explained what they were trying to do. How they wanted to help kids with limited opportunities and those who struggled with literacy. When he told his father about selling the Aston Martin, his father said, "Whatever you put in I'll match. It's a great cause."

"That's very generous and more than I expected."

His mother rose. "I'll leave you two alone to have a chat. I'm off to bed. Don't be long, darling."

Darling? He couldn't ever remember hearing his mother call his father anything other than Alexander. Perhaps his father's heart attack had made them both look at the life they led. They must have loved each other once. "Night, mom. Why don't you both come over for dinner one night soon." He was about to say that Stella would love to cook for them, but would she? She still hated the way his father treated Kendra when she had Connor.

His father's eyes welled with tears, and Marcus stiffened in shock. He'd never seen his father cry, and all the resentment and anger he'd held inside for his father dissolved. He would rather look to the future and leave the past behind. The future was scary enough.

"If I could do it all again, I would and I'd do it different—do it better. You both deserved more from me. Despite my worst efforts you've become such a success and I'm proud of you."

"It's largely due to the traits I inherited from you that I've succeeded. Stubborn, determined, never give up."

His father nodded. "But you've avoided making those habits turn you into a mini-dictator like I was. What I did to Kendra... I'm not sure I can forgive myself and your mother never will."

"At least you admit you were wrong. That takes guts, and I learned from your mistakes." He waited for his father to get angry, but the man merely laughed.

"Very true." His smile died as his father said, "But don't let that determination color what is best for you. Your sister tells me your back is so bad you need an operation, but you're pushing the doctor's advice aside. I know you're not stupid. What's holding you back?"

Bloody Tom must have blabbed. If anyone could understand his position, it would be his father. He explained the no-win situation he was in then sat back and waited.

"So, you want to wait until you can't handle the pain. Let me ask you this. How many pills are you popping a day? Not the amount Stella thinks you're taking but the truth."

He wanted to lie. He wanted to lie his ass off, but this was the first time his father had ever listened to him and he'd never lied to his father before. That's why they'd had so many arguments. They never agreed on anything. How could they, when they both advocated for different paths for Marcus's career?

"Yeah, I'm taking more than the Doc is recommending. I have to. The pain shooting down my legs is too much."

"I think you have your answer. No one is expecting you to be a hero, but you've never been afraid of anything in your life; not me, not racing, not Kendra's cancer. You never gave up. Yes, this operation has risks. It could have outcomes you don't like, but the longer you leave it the worse those outcomes become."

"It's all right for you. I might end up in a wheelchair or impotent."

"You'll still be alive and with the people who love you. You have enough money to make any adjustments you need to make, and the biggest reason of all is it might turn out fine and you'll live a wonderful life. You're such a fighter. I just know in my bones the operation is the right thing to do."

"What about Stella?"

His father frowned. "What about her?"

"What if I end up impotent? She wants children. What if I can't have children?"

"Didn't you just say you can freeze your sperm? You could also adopt. I can't really talk about children. I lost my children's respect because of my own terrible behavior. If she loves you, she will want to be with you, children or no children. Love forgives many sins. Look at your mother. How she put up with me for all these years... It had to be love."

"But is it fair on her to put Stella in this position?"

"That is not your decision to make, son. It's hers. If you love her, don't let your pride mess this up. Let her decide for herself. Isn't that what you wanted me to do? Let you make your decisions."

Marcus swallowed back his response. Pride was his middle name. He had the world at his feet and he didn't know how to be a person someone overlooked. How did he compete with the men who would go after Stella if he was in a wheelchair? What could he offer her? At the moment, he could offer her very little.

She didn't need his money. She could get any man she wanted for sex. She had the potential to destroy what little he did have left, his heart. If she walked out when things got too hard, he'd never get over losing her.

"Don't be afraid to love, Marcus. I've realized that nothing is more important in this life than love. Not money. Not power. Without love the world is a very lonely place."

His father was right, but Marcus hated feeling so vulnerable. He had so much to lose, and Stella had so little to gain in this relationship. Why did she love him? What did she see in him? With so many problems, she should run a mile.

"I'll think about what you have said."

"I won't push you, but if you want me to come with you to meet with Dr. Forrester again I will. We can get a second opinion. We'll find the best orthopedic surgeon in the world if we have to."

"Thanks, Dad. Shall I organize a meeting with Stella regarding the charity? We can wait until you've recuperated. I don't want to upset mom by working you too early. If you've got any ideas for other board members let me know."

"I'll put my thinking cap on. I have BMW America is one of

my clients. I'm sure I could get one of the senior managers there to come aboard."

"Fantastic. Thank you." He rose to leave. "Thank you for listening and for your words of advice and not pushing me into a decision. I appreciate that. Everyone else thinks they know best, but this is my life."

"Thank you for reaching out to mend a relationship I destroyed. You'll never know how much it means to me."

He leaned down and pressed a kiss to his father's cheek. "To new beginnings."

His father's eyes welled again. "New beginnings. I'm always here to listen if you need me."

As Marcus drove home in the old Dodge, he marveled at the meeting with his father. He couldn't wait to get home and tell Stella. Home and Stella were now completely intertwined, and it was a great feeling.

CHAPTER FIFTEEN

"She'll handle as smooth as silk if you treat her like you treat your women."

Marcus wanted to laugh at Sully's description of the Porsche Carrera the team had spent a month working on to make it faster, whilst maintaining solid control. "My woman has no complaints." Stella's face flashed into his mind. She was most definitely his woman, and warmth flooded his body. He was a lucky bastard.

"Are you sure your back's up to this?" Tom asked. "I can take her for a spin first."

A week on and his back felt better but... "Nope. That's my job. The customer wants to see the world champ behind the wheel of his car." Marcus had followed the Doc's orders as if he faced a death sentence. In a way, he did. Stella had threatened to leave if he didn't follow orders, and he didn't want that. He was well rested. He obsessively completed his daily physiotherapy, and he swum in the pool every night and he had his pills.

He'd taken his pain meds this morning, hence why he'd asked to test drive the car this early. He could do the drive before the pills wore off.

As he curled up to slide behind the wheel, his back spasmed and he gritted his teeth. Shit, it shouldn't hurt this bad getting into the bucket seat. He reached to pull on the safety harness and drew in a sharp breath as once again pain stabbed down his spine.

His mind blocked the pain as he revved the engine. He loved the deep, power filled purr of a Porsche. He eased the throttle and took it for a few gentle warm up laps. Carlos, the owner, sat in the stand. That's the perk they offered. The owner got to watch the ex-formula one world champ drive their car around a racetrack. He had a show to put on as well as ensuring the car met the customer's brief.

He felt the extra power as he tapped the accelerator. He grinned inside his helmet as he let the power surround him. The team had done an amazing job. Sully really knew his stuff, and he was thankful they'd given him shares in the business. They couldn't lose him.

He pushed hard on the accelerator and demanded more speed. He tightened his grip on the steering wheel to keep control of the power, and as he did, pain ripped through his body and sweat dripped into his eyes. He blinked a few times to clear his vision. As the hairpin bend approached fast, he tightened his grip, double clutched and... *fuck.* He almost blacked out momentarily from the pain. His vision dimmed, and he hit the bend too fast.

The car spun out of control and it took his remaining consciousness to avoid hitting the wall. He didn't want to destroy his customer's car. As the blackness took over completely, he brought the car to a stop.

"Be careful getting him out. He's got a bad back."

Through a dark haze, Tom's voice sounded so panicked he wanted to laugh. So he did.

"Jeez, Marcus. What the hell? I thought you'd died behind that wheel."

He wasn't dead. He was on the blacktop of the racetrack, wracked with pain. "Pain can't kill you, but it makes you faint sometimes. I hope the car's okay. I'd better talk to Carlos."

He tried to stand, but decided that was a very bad idea. Seven weeks' worth of resting his back had come undone with one drive. They didn't make those seats for a man as tall as him with a fucked up back. Fear inched its way up his body. If he couldn't drive the cars, their whole business model was at risk. What did he bring to the party? He was no mechanic.

"Do you need a hand up?" Tom asked.

"Give me a minute."

"I'll talk to Carlos. I've checked the car, and it's fine. That was an amazing piece of driving to miss the wall in the chicane."

He ignored Sully's praise because he clenched his teeth as more pain hit. If he didn't know any better, he'd suspect Dr. Forrester had given him sugar candies instead of pain meds and no amount of mind over matter was going to see him getting off the ground soon.

He heard Sully walk off.

Tom crouched down next to him. "It's getting worse, Marcus. I'm not happy about keeping this from Kendra."

"You haven't because she told father."

Tom ignored him. "I know Stella's worried too. Have the surgery. If you'd been driving on the freeway and crashed... I'm scared to let you have Connor or Matti in your car."

His fists clenched at his side, and he pushed himself up on his elbows, sweat beading his forehead again. "I just need more time." More time with Stella before he had to let her go. He wasn't afraid of the operation even though it would might leave him less of a man, but he was afraid of trapping Stella. She might say she could live with him in a wheelchair, but reality was never like it was in the movies or on TV. What if he couldn't make love to her again? She loved sex. It was the one thing that originally drew them together. *Erectile dysfunction could occur.'* Dr. Forrester's words echoed in his ears and his balls shriveled.

No one understood the Sophie's choice he faced; operation or no operation. Pain for life, or spending it as a cripple with no sex life.

There would be no winners in this choice.

"Time is not on your side, bro." Tom stood, shaking his head. "I'll ring Stella and get her to come get you."

"No. Absolutely not. She's got an important meeting today. The ball is in a few days." He rolled onto his side like his physio-therapist had taught him and moved onto all fours, trying to ignore his shaking arms, and pushed into a standing position. He beamed as if he was a trained monkey who could stand at his master's command. "I've got to meet with the accountant about Miami."

"Do you think we should put Miami on hold until your back's sorted?"

Probably, but he wasn't about to admit that. He needed something to take his mind off his back or he'd go crazy.

"We can talk about it later. I've gotta go."

THE MEETING HAD GONE WELL. THE ACCOUNTANT APPROVED THE cash-flow forecast for the Miami project. They just needed to find the right location. What he wanted now was two little pills to make it through the rest of the afternoon, but he had three hours to go yet.

What had he said to Tom, *pain couldn't kill you?* He had his doubts about that statement now. If he went home, Stella would see how much pain he was in.

Not wanting to go home was a terrible sign, but on the other hand, Stella would be there to take the pain away. They'd talked about Miami and Stella was fine to go with him as long as it wasn't longer than two years. He'd fallen in love with her even more at her sacrifice. Her reasoning was she didn't have a job and she could fly back and forth for her charity work.

He gave in and popped more pills.

She was his only bright light in a dark day and, as always, the thought of her gave him hope to face the future, but also terrified him, because it could end. If he told her the truth, she'd be silly not to consider leaving him.

She was such a beautiful soul. Would she leave him if he became less of a man?

Part of him hung on to the knowledge she might stay, but she would have to love him to do that, and while she said she did, she'd basically told him it was over in Maui because she was looking for Mr. Right, and obviously she hadn't considered him. He was a coward. Tell her the truth. *Bastard.* Hiding his condition wasn't fair to her. He parked his car in the underground garage, and like a man of eighty, he eased slowly out of the seat, and wished with all his heart things were different. The idea of losing her scared him as much as losing the use of his legs.

Pain ricocheted around his body as he straightened.

He called Stella's name as he entered the apartment, and his pain lessened when he heard her voice. "Hey, babe, wanna join me in the shower?" He stopped as he walked into his lounge and came face to face with Kendra, Tom, Sully, Lexi, Kade, and Stella. "What the fuck…"

"Yes, it's an intervention," his sister said as she rose with hands on hips. "Tom told me what happened today at the track and don't you dare look at him like that. You should have told me months ago and so should have Stella. I thought she was my best friend."

Stella sighed and threw her arms up in the air. "It's not that simple, Kendra."

"It is that simple. My brother could have been killed on that track today. I want to know what's going on and what's happening." To his horror, his sister burst into tears.

He crossed the room fighting the anger, realizing these people loved him and were as worried as he was. He pulled his sister into an embrace. "Sssh. Don't cry, sis."

"I almost lost you to one crash. I won't lose you to another." He watched Stella's face over his sister's head and her eyes filled with tears, too. She turned away from his probing gaze.

"I'll make us some coffee," Stella said, and left the room as if a bad smell was following her.

"My wife is right," said Tom. "Until your back mends you can't test drive for us."

He scrubbed his hand across his face. Tiredness was a bitch. "Then who? It's one of our major competitive edges to have a Formula One driver."

"Jason could do it," Kade uttered.

Silence descended, and he fought his rising fury.

"Before you get all pissed, think about it. Jason could contract to drive until your back's sorted, that's all. He might not have been the world champion, but he was a well thought of driver and won a few races."

He wished he could punch Kade for suggesting his own brother, but times were desperate. He could throw a hissy fit, or pull a pity party, but all these people had trusted him and gone into business with him at Bad Boy Autos. He couldn't do anything to fuck with that. Their livelihoods depended on this business. "Only until my back is better."

Once again, silence descended. Then Kendra cried, "Christ, how bad is it? You'd never let Jason near your cars unless your life depended on it." She turned and moved towards the kitchen. "Stella, get your ass in here."

Stella arrived carrying a tray of coffees and set it on the occasional table. She came to stand beside him and took his hand in hers. "Let's all sit and Marcus can explain the situation."

She squeezed his hand, and when he looked into her eyes, he knew his moment had come. He would have to admit he needed surgery, but he couldn't bring himself to share the risks or what might become of the man they saw in front of them.

He let go of Stella's hand and took the chair sitting away from the rest of them. He ignored the hurt on Stella's face. If he was going to do this, he would do it his way and on his terms. He couldn't use Stella as his crutch. He would set her free. She'd hurt to begin with, but that hurt would fade. What he couldn't bear was her by his bedside, learning he'd become half a man and watching as her need for him melted away.

He had his pride. He didn't want a woman who was only with him because of pity or out of a sense of duty.

"Two of my discs have degenerated. Dr. Forrester suggested surgery almost a year ago. My pain levels, as you saw today, are unmanageable long term. The surgery may involve removal and replacement of the whole, or a part, of the affected discs Another option is a spinal fusion that reduces the movement in my damaged spine area."

"Is the operation risky?" Lexie asked, biting her bottom lip. "It sounds kinda scary."

He looked at Stella. She spoke for him. "Yes. I think that's why Marcus held out for so long, but he won't tell me more." The accusation hung in the air.

He ignored her comment. "The recuperation time is long. I could be in hospital for up to a week and on my back or restricted movement only for three to four weeks and then up to six months of physiotherapy." He hung his head. "There is no guarantee that I'll be pain free either." He absolutely would not tell them he might need ongoing surgery and could end up crippled, in a wheelchair, incontinent, and no longer able to get a hard on. That was his own private hell.

"But what are the risks?" Tom pressed.

He shrugged. "The same risk as any surgery. Any time you go under the knife there are risks."

"So, there's no risk you'll be paralyzed?"

Trust bloody Lexie to ask. He watched the fear spread across Kendra's face and wished Lexie had kept her mouth shut.

"That's why you're prepared to live with this pain, isn't it? You might be paralyzed," Kendra said and burst into another round of tears.

"Come on, Kendra. Tears are not helping. You've seen what the pain is doing to him. Do you think he is deciding to do this for fun? He no longer has a choice if he wants to lead an active life. Don't let your fear take away his choices." Stella spoke the truth. She looked at him. Her eyes filled with something that looked a lot like love, and he wanted to pull her into his arms and let her take his pain and fear away. "It's Marcus's life and his decision. Only he knows how much pain he can take and whether surgery is worth the risk. Either way, I'm sure we'll all be here for him whatever his decision and whatever the outcome."

He realized what he'd seen. Love. Could she really love him? Or did he imagine it? If it was true, there would also be the devotion from her love for him. She'd stand by him no matter what, and the thought of her having to look after the shell of the man he could become made bile rise. He would not do that to her. Could not do that to her. What was the saying? If you loved someone, set them free.

His father had suggested letting Stella decide for herself, but she had too good a heart to leave him if the worst happened. A part of him wanted to bet on that.

"Of course, we'll be here for you. We can manage the business. We're booked for the next eight months, and if Colter is free to test drive for us, then now would be a good time," said Sully, always the sensible one.

"Listen. I appreciate the concern. I have some thinking to do and I need to talk to Dr. Forrester, so why don't you all go home and I promise to keep you updated." When none of them moved, he added, "I really need to lie down. My back's killing me." He laughed, but no one laughed with him. Shit, this was how it was going to be.

Kade rose and pulled Lexie to her feet with him. "It sounds like you and Stella have some talking to do." He held out his hand, and Marcus shook it. "You know where we are if you need us."

"Later, man." Sully left, too.

Kendra didn't look like she was going anywhere. Marcus pointed to the balcony. "Tom, let's get some air. I need to catch up on what Carlos thought about today."

"TELL ME ALL OF IT, RIGHT NOW." KENDRA HAD EVERY RIGHT TO be mad, but Stella didn't know what more to tell her.

"He hasn't told me anything that he didn't tell you just now."

Kendra stood and paced. "There has to be a way we can find out what his prognosis is. What if we spoke to Dr. Forrester?"

Stella shook her head. "I've tried that, and he's all about patient confidentiality, which I fully understand. Marcus would sue his ass off if he told us about his case."

Kendra swung round. "That's it. What if it's not questions about Marcus's case, just a hypothetical case?"

She could hug her friend. "Great idea, but he may still feel this is surfing close to the wind. We could only ask broad questions."

"We have to try." Kendra pleaded.

"I agree. I have this feeling Marcus is holding something back. I'm too scared to push because everything is going so well."

"Can't be going that well if he's not confiding in you."

Her friend was right. "I'll set up a meeting." She held up her hand as Kendra opened her mouth. "And I won't tell Marcus, but you can't tell Tom either."

Kendra hugged her. "Deal. Once we learn more, we'll know how best to help him. I hate seeing him in this pain. My brother thinks he has to be the best at everything and it's almost like it's a personal goal to prove he doesn't need surgery and that he can endure the pain. Idiot. The pain won't go away because Marcus decrees it."

She hoped that was all it was. Marcus was many things, but he wasn't a stupid man. If the surgery could improve his life, why wouldn't he go ahead? Agreeing to let Colter drive for him, screamed that something else was going on and the worry ate at her stomach.

He was hiding something and while that frightened her, what hurt her more was that if they were supposed to be in a relationship, why didn't he share it with her?

It made her doubt his heart was really committed to making this work and perhaps she was merely convenient as a nurse-maid and bed pal.

"I'll ring Dr. Forrester now."

CHAPTER SIXTEEN

K endra and Stella sat in Dr. Forrester's office the next day, late in the afternoon. Stella had told Marcus she had last-minute shopping to do for the ball.

"I realize you can't reveal anything about a specific patient's condition, but we have a few questions about degenerate disc disease and we were hoping you could answer them for us."

Dr. Forrester was nearing his mid-fifties and had the kindest eyes she'd ever seen. Those eyes looked at them, and it was obvious he knew why they were here. He sighed.

"This is very tricky for me, ladies. Your questions would have to be pretty broad. To be honest, most of your questions can be answered by googling. Everything you need to know is on my website."

"Then you wouldn't be in trouble for clarifying some of those website points," Kendra pushed.

"Perhaps." He took his glasses off and cleaned them. "I'll answer what I can."

The frank and honest conversation lasted about thirty minutes, and both women's faces looked as if they'd seen a ghost by the time they'd finished.

"Holy shit." Kendra whispered as they took the elevator down to basement parking garage.

Why didn't Marcus tell me? This was major surgery with major repercussions. Many of which affected her too. All Stella could think about was Marcus hadn't trusted her. Why hadn't he fully explained his situation? Did he think she'd leave him? He was asking her to try for a permanent life with him, yet he wasn't being truthful about what kind of life they might face. Her stomach heaved, and she wished she had anywhere else to go than back to face Marcus. She needed time to process this news and what it meant for her, for him, and for them.

No wonder he was reluctant to have the operation. *Paralysis. Wheelchair. Impotency.* Dr. Forrester had explained these were worse case scenarios, and there were several options should any of these conditions occur. Options? They all sounded terrible.

"If you can't handle this, you have to leave him now. Now, before he learns you know the truth."

"I'm not leaving."

Kendra pulled her round to face her. "Did you hear those words? I know you always think everything will turn out okay, but what if it doesn't? I know you. You're not a pushing a wheelchair kinda girl. You're a party animal. Fun, sun, and sex. All of which you could lose if you stay with Marcus."

"That is so unfair." She stepped back from her friend. A friend she'd sat through months of illness with as a teenager. A friend she'd never deserted. Tears welled. "How can you say that to me? I don't desert my friends when they're in need. You of all people know that." Let alone her charity work. "Yes, I have a trust fund large enough to never have to worry. That's one thing Marcus likes; I don't care about his money. I won't apologize for living my life to the full because guess what? Your illness taught me that. It also taught me to go after what you want in life, as it's short. And I love Marcus. I want a life with him no matter what that life looks like."

She stood, breathing heavily. She did. Christ. *She really did.* She loved him. "I love him. Would you walk away from Tom if the worst happened?"

Kendra burst into tears and sunk to the ground in the underground carpark. "No way. I'm sorry. It's just... you love life. You love sex. I could never keep up with who you were sleeping with. Can you imagine what's going through Marcus's head? Can you imagine what he might do if he couldn't..."

She crouched down next to Kendra. "We have to be strong. We have to make him see he has no choice. Did you hear what Dr. Forrester said? If one of the disc's ruptures and damages the spinal cord, he could be paralyzed."

"What are we going to do?" Kendra sobbed, and Stella didn't know what to say.

"One thing we don't have to worry about is money. Whatever happens we can afford to pay for the best treatment and rehabilitation and that's more than many in his situation." Stella was already thinking of those less fortunate. A charity event idea took hold, but it would have to wait. "You know your brother. Who will he listen to? Who can get through to him? I obviously can't sway him. He won't even tell me the truth."

Kendra slowly pushed herself up, using the concrete pillar until she was standing again. "He might listen to Sully. Tom's out because he's married to me. Marcus would never tell Tom anything because he knows Tom would tell me."

Like a tidal wave, relief swamped her. "You're right. He'd listen to Sully. Everyone listens to Sully. Let's go home via Bad Boy Autos and have a little talk with him."

"What are you going to say to Marcus when you get home?"

Kendra's question knotted her stomach again. "I don't know. I don't know if I should try to talk to him or leave it to Sully. Do I even tell him I know?" What she really wanted to do was talk about their trust situation, or lack thereof. What sort of relationship did Marcus want if he couldn't talk to her about something as life changing as this?

"Whatever you decide, please try to remember what he must be going through. How afraid he must be."

"I'm not exactly dancing about all of this." Her stomach clenched tighter than a pair of nun's knickers. "I would have thought if we are a proper couple he'd have talked to me about it so that we'd get through it together. Like you and Tom."

As they slid into Stella's car, Kendra reminded her, "Like Tom and I? Don't you remember when I thought the cancer had come back? I pushed Tom away. Until you face things like this, you don't know how you'll react. Maybe he's protecting himself, but more likely he thinks he's protecting you. If it was you having this operation, how would you act?"

She hadn't thought about it like that. With a sigh she said, "I'd want Marcus to have choices. I wouldn't want to trap him if I couldn't live a full life, but I'd also be petrified he'd leave me if he knew too."

Is that how Marcus felt? Scared to tell her? Or would he try to push her away to protect her from what may come?

She might not be able to discuss his condition, but she could ask him about their relationship and where he saw it going. If he didn't confess about the operation, where did it leave her? Where did it leave them? She wouldn't live like his mother, with his father leading and making the decisions. She wanted a true partnership. She didn't want to invest her heart any further if he wasn't in the game.

"You ladies have been busy." Sully sat in the break room of Bad Boy Autos, sipping his iced-coffee.

"Someone has to help Marcus. Everyone needs someone to

lean on when things are bad." How could Sully not see that? He'd taken the news so calmly Stella wanted to shake him.

"True. When I hit rock bottom with my drinking, I had no one until I went to my first AA meeting. Then my world changed. I had people who understood my situation and who supported me." He rubbed his chin. "Do they have an association or group for fucked backs?"

Stella smiled at Sully's joke. "You never know. I bet there is some sort of group," and she got out her mobile and started googling. "What do you know? www.Spinenation.com."

Kendra piped in and added, "There's also the www.arthristis.org."

"If he stays on these bloody pills any longer, he'll need Narcotics Anonymous. Sully, you are the only one who can understand why I can't let that happen."

Sully merely nodded. "Of course you realize he has to want to sort this out. He has to want to help himself."

"Speaking from experience."

"Absolutely." Sully reached across the table and squeezed Stella's hand. "You know Marcus and what happened with his father. The harder his father pushed, the harder Marcus resisted or did the opposite. If you push him, he'll dig his toes in."

"So we do nothing?"

"You could be right about talking to him. He needs to have someone that can listen. A friend to talk through this with and someone who doesn't take sides. You're too close."

"It's not about taking sides. It's about trying to help him. Dr. Forrester said the longer he waits the worse the spinal cord damage will be and if a disc ruptures... he could become paralyzed. If I can prevent that, I will." Stella's heart beat faster, fear rising, but she swallowed it back down.

"Fretting won't help anyone. I'll swing by tonight. Can you arrange to be out?"

"Come to mine and advise me on my outfit for the ball."

"Good thinking, Kendra." Stella smiled. "I'll bring over those earrings you like."

"Now we've got that sorted, best you let me get on with my work or Marcus will ask me what I've been doing all day."

"Has he been in the office today?"

He flashed Stella a smile. "Yes, this morning. I think he's pushing on with the Miami thing. He's talking about visiting after the ball."

Stella's mouth dropped open. "He's in no condition to go flying off to Miami. He can barely get out of bed at the moment."

"You're right. He has his head in the sand or up his ass. He could barely walk this morning. I'll talk to him. I promise."

Kendra remained silent.

"Are you okay?" Sully asked.

"Not really. My brother is living in excruciating pain, and now I know why. He's scared and I don't know how to help him."

"Just be there for him." Stella hugged her. "That's all we could do for you and it helped, didn't it?"

Kendra nodded.

"Go home, both of you. Worrying won't change Marcus's mind. I'll see what I can do but don't expect miracles. Sometimes a person has to come to terms in their own time."

"Trouble is, I think he's run out of time."

STELLA COULD HEAR A WOMAN'S HUSKY LAUGH AS SHE LET herself into Marcus's apartment late in the afternoon. She thought nothing of it until she walked into the living room to see Marcus standing by the massage table, naked except for a towel wrapped round his waist. Worse still, a woman with short red painted fingernails stroked his arm as if he were her new pet. Of course her chest had to be the size of a pair of watermelons, and Marcus's eyes definitely were most definitely not looking at her face.

His beaming smile cooled when he saw her.

"Stella, darling. Come and meet Mandy. She's filling in while Julie is on holiday."

She'd relaxed when she'd learned Marcus's daily physiotherapist was a fifty-five-year-old grandmother called Julie. However, Mandy was nowhere near fifty, more like twenty-five, and just the type of eye-candy Marcus usually loved. Big boobs, legs that went on forever and plumped up lips that could suck-start a van.

"Lovely to meet you, Mandy. How's the patient today?"

Mandy eyed her up and down as if sizing up the competition. Little did she know Marcus was off the market. Mandy looked at Marcus, almost drooling over his pecs. "It's only his amazing core strength that makes him able to walk at all if you ask me."

"I keep saying he needs to consider surgery, but will he listen to me?" Stella replied as she moved close and wrapped her arms around his waist. The bloody man loved it too. He loved seeing the green-eyed monster rise in her eyes.

"Mandy, I'll show you out. Same time tomorrow. I need to ensure my back's as good as it can be for the ball tomorrow night."

Stella didn't release him. "Why don't you have a shower, sweetheart? I'll show Mandy out."

"That's okay, I'll show myself out. I just need to pack away the table." Mandy bent over and picked up the towels.

"Leave everything. You're back tomorrow morning, anyway. Stella can throw those in the washer."

She knew exactly where she wanted to throw them and it wouldn't be into the washer. He was enjoying this like a dog with a juicy bone.

"Okay. I'll see you tomorrow." Mandy gave Marcus a brazen smile that left him in no doubt she'd love to see a whole lot more of him tomorrow.

As soon as the door closed behind Mandy, Marcus burst out laughing. "You should see your face. It's as green as grass."

"Maybe it's because you couldn't take your eyes off her double F chest," said Stella folding her arms across her barely-there-at-all chest.

Marcus's laughter died and he pulled her into an embrace. "Oh, honey, your tits are perfect for me. I love every inch of you. Real is far better than fake." When she remained unresponsive in his arms, he added, "You had no problem with Julie. Mandy is simply a physio too."

"Right. So if you walked in on me naked in a towel with a guy drooling over me, you'd be okay?"

He hugged her tighter. "Shit, no. I take your point." He remained silent. "Want me to ring and ask for another physiotherapist?"

Finally, she wrapped her arms around him. "No." *This was the perfect time.* "I guess we have to learn to trust each other in this relationship."

"I do trust you, and you know you can trust me. I never lie. You know that."

Honest! He's lying by omission. He was honest to a fault, but he obviously considered not telling her everything wasn't a lie. She wanted to ask him about the operation and Dr. Forrester, but she'd promised Sully she's wait until he'd talked to Marcus.

"So, neither of us has any reason to be jealous." She smiled at him. "Because I intend to dance at the ball, and I'll have to dance with all the donors. So I expect you to behave."

His grip on her waist tightened. "You love dancing and I'll not be up for it. I'm not much use in the bedroom at the moment either. Sometimes I wonder why you want to be with me? What do we have in common?"

She stilled in his embrace. At last some heartfelt truth. He was expressing his fear. She wished she knew what to say. "We have our shit upbringings to bond over. We have our friends and your sister. We have the same joy in life. Same values. A fantastic sex life. The same wants and needs, I hope. And we have love. We have each other."

"Is that enough? How on earth can I be Mr. Right like this or am I merely Mr. Right for now. "

She stepped out of his embrace. "What we share is more than enough, and your sister says there is no such thing as Mr. Right. More like Mr. He's The One, warts and all. I'm not after perfection. Perfection gets boring quickly."

"What if I can't..." He stopped, and she held her breath. *Say more.. Tell me...* "Never mind." He looked down at her. "I need a shower to wash off all the massage oil." He wiggled his eyebrows. "Care to join me?"

She stroked his muscled chest. "How can I decline such a tempting offer Mr. Black?"

"This is where I'd swing you into my arms but you know swinging is out for me at the moment."

She wrapped her arms around his neck. "I'm quite capable of walking, and I'd walk, or I'd crawl, anywhere with you, for you." She kissed him. Kissed him with all the love that was in her heart. She wanted him to realize she'd never leave him, no matter what happened. Maybe then he'd open up to her and let her in. If he couldn't... would he always keep a part of himself from her? What else might he never share? Would that be enough for her?

He kissed her back as if his life depended on it, and she soared to dizzying heights. They could work. What ever happened in their lives, if they just trusted in their love for each other. Would he love her enough to share everything?

She broke the kiss and they stood smiling at each other. So

many unsaid words hung in the air. Finally she moved. "Come on. Let's get you soaped up."

"I like the sound of that," he said.

She took his hand and led him towards the ensuite in their bedroom. She turned the power jets of the shower on. "I love the size of this shower with all the shower heads."

"I had it especially made when I redecorated the apartment."

She laughed. "I should have known. It's a shower built for two." She eyed him as she removed her clothes. "Knowing you, they made it for three or four."

"Nope." He moved closer and dropped his towel, making her eyes water at the sight of his erection. She knew exactly what she was going to do with that, but before she could, he used his finger to lift her face until she was only looking into his eyes. "I've always been a one woman at a time guy. I've never needed more, and now I'm a one special woman only guy. My Stella." He leaned in and pressed a kiss to her lips. "Only you."

Her heart bloomed in her chest as he led her under the water. She'd never wanted him more. His hands roamed her body, squeezing her breasts, and one hand moved down between her legs. She moaned as he stroked her. He knew exactly how to touch her, to make her come far too quickly.

She kept her eyes open, even though water was streaming everywhere. She loved looking at him. You'd never know the condition of his back or the pain he fought each day. He was a magnificent male specimen, all muscles and hard edges. His ink rippled as he moved and the water seemed to lick him.

But it was his eyes that drew her. His eyes were where the real Marcus hid. She could see the little boy who had to prove to his father that he was the best because otherwise his father would win. She saw the man who had helped his sister fight a demon no one could see. She saw the man who thought mind over matter would fix his back. She saw the fear hidden there that he could lose everything if he didn't win the war.

It didn't take long for her to come apart. Her heart loved him, and she'd been wet for him before the towel came off. Her body wanted more, but she knew his back wouldn't take it. She could wait. He didn't have to.

She dropped to her knees and cupped his balls. They were tight with need. She ran a finger up and down the length of him, and he leaned back against the shower wall, his eyes hooded as he watched her. "God, you are so beautiful," he whispered.

"So are you," she murmured as she licked from his balls to the tip of his penis. She loved how the muscles in the thighs she gripped quivered. She worked her tongue over the slit at the end. His taste was always so male. He groaned and his hands flattened against the tiles. She loved the taste of him. She loved the feel of him and how the hard managed to get even harder at her touch.

Slowly she took the long, long length of him into her mouth, inch by inch, and once she could take no more she sucked, hard. His eyes closed and his head hit the tiled wall behind him.

"You make me want to come too soon."

She smiled and then she moved her mouth further on him. His hips flexed, and he went deeper. She loved giving him head. It made her feel so powerful to have this giant of a man at her mercy. She decided when he could come, not him.

She wrapped her hand around the base of him and soon her mouth and hand worked him until his legs shook, so she eased back, letting him slip from her mouth. She licked his balls and cock until he begged.

"Tease. I so want to come, please…" His hand found her hair and he gripped tight. "More," he demanded as he guided her back to his straining cock, and she laughed.

"So impatient. Relax and enjoy."

"Relax? I'm wound tighter than an archer's bow." But his grip on her hair loosened and she took him back into her mouth.

She worked him well. His hands, still in her hair, guided her, showing her what he needed, and the rhythm he enjoyed the most. She continued to tease him, taking him to the edge and then back again several more times until his groans filled the shower stall, drowning out the sound of the water hitting their heated bodies. His strong thighs held him up until he screamed her name as he came.

She walked her way back up his body with lips and hands, loving the sound of his thundering heart under her ear. She loved this man, and it was clear that it didn't matter to her what sort of life they had as long as it was together. Wasn't that what the marriage vows said? For better, for worse. True love wasn't selfish and nowhere did it say *I'm only here for the good times*.

"God, Stella. What you do to me," he gasped.

"Is your back okay?"

"I'm fine, sweetheart. The wall helped. What about you? Can this really be enough for you? You love sex. Sex brought us together."

"But it's not just about the sex with us anymore. It's about hopes and dreams. You know what I want—children, a family. You said you want that too."

"I do. With you. But my back—"

—"Being with you is enough. We'll make this work. Looking at you makes me wet, and you always know how to get me off with a simple touch. Anything more can wait until you're better." His mouth firmed, before he opened it, but no words came out so she told him, "What we share is enough. I swear."

The tight lines round his mouth didn't relax, and she wished she could convince him she was happy. She'd be happier if he opened up and let her help him. He needed her to do and say the right things so he'd have the bloody operation. Then they would know what they faced, and they'd face it together. She wasn't going anywhere.

"If you're happy to do all the work, let's spend the rest of the day and night in bed. We can watch those old movies you love, eat ice cream, and when my back's rested you can ride me until your toes curl."

Sully's coming round. "I have to help Kendra with her outfit for the ball tomorrow night." She pressed a kiss to his chest. "How about we have a late supper in bed and I'll bring some Ben and Jerry's Phish Food home? You rest that back."

"Bloody hell. I loathe being a fucking invalid." His arms tightened around her. "Do you have to go? I've hardly seen you this week with all the ball stuff."

"It'll be over tomorrow night. Then I'll be all yours for a while. You'll probably be sick of me by the end of next week."

Her heart sank when he didn't deny her statement. He turned off the water and gingerly stepped out. The scar on his back was red from the hot shower. He held out a towel and wrapped her in it, pulling her in close. "I love having you here."

Love flooded her heart, and she relaxed into his arms. It was moments like this that made all the worry and doubts worth it.

"Don't stay too long at Kendra's. I'm hungry, but not for food."

He at least let her dry his lower half so he didn't have to bend.

"I'll be back soon. Put the electric blanket on and relax your muscles while I'm gone and I'll give you a massage when I get back, but it won't be the type of massage Mandy gives you."

CHAPTER SEVENTEEN

H is apartment always seemed empty when Stella left. How could he have lived on his own for so long? Maybe because he just needed the right woman to share his life with. Stella was becoming his Mrs. Right.

He laid back on the bed and let the pain meds he'd just popped do their job. She'd throw a complete fit when she found out he had a secret stash. He'd been given an extra prescription by the asshat Andy at the hospital in Maui. He'd tried hard to do the two in the morning and two in the evening regime, but since the test drive of Carlos's car, he'd needed more.

With Stella sharing his bed, they were careful to use positions that didn't strain his back, but sometimes the slightest movement knifed through him. Soon he wouldn't be able to perform at all. And then what?

Stella wasn't an abstinence kind of woman. As for him, if he lost his ability to have sex, would life be worth living?

Stella checked his bottle from Dr. Forrester, but she didn't know about the other bottle. She thought he managed on four pills a day when it was really more like eight to ten.

He tried to push away the guilt. He wasn't exactly lying to

her, but he *was* hiding things from her. He wanted to confide in her, but she'd push him to have the op and then what?

Staying with him wouldn't be a picnic should the worst happen.

The worst might not happen.

If the doctors could give him certainty, he knew he'd have the operation tomorrow.

He was in a quandary. Many people held on to life through pain and suffering because of this uncertainty.

He ran a hand across his face.

He was getting pretty tired of the pain.

He was getting pretty tired of the pretense he could manage.

He was just getting pretty tired.

His mobile pinged. It was a text message from Sully. *'At the door, bro'*

He thought he could rest his back for the few hours Stella would be at Kendra's. *'On my way'*, he texted back.

"Hi, Sully, come on in. Want a beer?"

Sully nodded as he closed the door behind him and followed Marcus into the kitchen.

"Did I catch you sleeping, boss? You took a while to get to the door." He hated it when Sully called him boss. Sully was almost forty-three years old and wiser than Tom and Marcus combined. A recovering alcoholic, he'd been sober for almost sixteen years and he was also the best auto-electrician on the West Coast.

"Sort of. Just resting." He handed his head mechanic a Bud and grabbed one for himself. "Is everything okay at the garage? Lexie's back from honeymoon, so you should have plenty of staff. Zip's not taking his leave for another month."

"It's cool. We've got two Porsches in next week that Lexie's working on. It's hard to get her to concentrate though. She's been raving about a restored vintage Jaguar 1950 XK120 Roadster she drove in New Zealand."

Marcus spun round to face him. "Shit. Really? I've been looking for one of those for years. Is it for sale?"

"I don't know. Ask her."

"I could fly down to New Zealand and check it out," he said, ignoring Sully.

"Don't be bloody stupid. You're in no condition to fly anywhere. How would you even test drive it?" Sully shook his head and headed towards the living room, grabbing a spot on the sofa while Marcus stood. Standing was better than sitting. He leaned against the pillar by the dining table.

"You could go for me."

Sully pointed a finger at him. "So, you're finally admitting your back's fucked. Then why aren't you doing something about it?"

Marcus let the fire in his gut rise. "Is that why you're bloody here? Did Tom ask you to talk to me? No! I bet it was Kendra."

"They're concerned about you and to be honest so am I. I know it's bad because your eyes were like pinpricks today and they still are. Stella says you're only taking two pills in the morning and two at night but that's bullshit. You're as high as a kite, and this opiate use has been going on for a while." Marcus was about to deny everything when Sully added. "I know how destructive addiction can be. It cost me my wife and children. If you don't want to hurt Stella, then tell me what the fuck is going on and why you're being a pussy about this operation?"

"I can't have this conversation here. I need to lie down. If you want to talk, you'll have to do it in my bedroom."

"There's a phrase I never thought I'd hear from you."

Marcus laughed. "This is what I've come to, begging men to come to my bedroom."

"You don't have to beg. I'm happy to listen and help where I can."

Once he was lying on the bed and Sully was in the chair by

the window, he said, "Do you want the short version or the long."

"Just tell me what's going on in that stubborn head of yours."

Marcus told Sully everything; the risks, the different outcomes that could happen, and Dr. Forrester recommendations. "The odds aren't good because of where the damaged discs are."

"Shit. Tough break man. You've every right to be scared and cautious, but you know something that's pissing me off."

"What?"

"You've promised something to Stella. You've dangled a relationship in front of her, but you're too chickenshit to be truthful with her. She deserves to know what she's getting in to. Solid relationships aren't built on lies. I should know. I lied through my teeth and lost any chance of a reconciliation with my family."

"If I tell her everything I might lose her anyway."

"That's not your choice to make. It's hers. You know deep inside that you can't go on like this. Have the surgery. The longer you leave it the more damage may occur."

"It's easy for you to say. You're not looking at ending up in a wheelchair with a limp cock." Anger scored his words, and he wished he could throw something at Sully's smug face.

"Keep popping these pills, let your discs blow out and you'll end up in a wheelchair with a limp cock and you'll be alone. You think you can control the pills? Let me tell you, you can't. No one is that strong. Not even the world-famous Marcus Black. You're kidding yourself if you think these pills don't come at a cost. The question is what, or who, are you prepared to lose?"

"Stella deserves so much more than me. She's so full of life. I couldn't bear to bind her to a cripple or worse."

"That's her decision."

"That's what my father said. I want to believe you. You know she'd never leave me if something bad happened. She hasn't got it in her to be disloyal. She'd think it her duty to stay."

"Probably, but I think it's because she loves you."

He turned to look at Sully. "What? She broke up with me to look for Mr. Right."

"Christ, you're an idiot. She broke up with you because you were her Mr. Right but you couldn't see it."

Marcus's body went into hyper-drive, the blood singing in his veins. "Why didn't she tell me?"

Sully shrugged. "Too scared you'd run for the hills, or should I say hobble." He laughed at his own joke. "How the two of you think you're having a relationship when you can't even tell each other how you feel is beyond me." He stood. "Tell her everything. She'll either stay or go, but either way you'll know where you stand, or lie, in your case. You'll still have me, Tom and Kendra to get you through this operation."

"Gee. It's easy for you to say, but not so easy to do. It could change my life forever."

Sully nodded. "Yip. It could actually make it better, have you considered that?"

He'd tried not to get his hopes up, be prepared for the worst so he could handle it.

"I'll tell her after the ball. I don't want to lay this on her the day before such an important event."

"That sounds fair. Have faith in the woman you love."

"How did you know?"

"Of course you love her. Why else are you so scared of losing her?" He picked up Marcus's empty beer can as he took his leave. "I'll show myself out."

Marcus lay back on the bed, his mind whirling. He was a risk taker. You didn't drive in Formula One without being able to analyze risk and make a calculated decision. Why did the idea of confessing everything scare him so much? Sully's words were right. This thing with Stella could only go two ways. It would finish or they would move forward.

He wasn't sure what he was more afraid of. If she left, he'd be devastated, but then it wouldn't matter if he had the surgery or not. If she stayed, the outcome mattered greatly.

It was going to be a long twenty-four hours. Once the ball was over, he would have the heart to heart with Stella. To prove he wasn't a pussy, he picked up his cell and dialed.

"Dr. Forrester, please." He waited. "Hi, Doc… no, everything's fine. I want to book a time to come in and discuss having this operation."

As he hung up from a very pleased Dr. Forrester, having made an appointment for ten on Thursday, he tried not to let the fear take him. Every race car driver had a healthy respect for fear. It kept you sharp, helped you make the right decisions in an instant.

As the sun began to fade, in the darkening room, he prayed he was making the right decision.

He rolled over to get to his feet. He needed a piss. Pain shafted down his leg and he bit back a groan. *Fuck.* He *was* out of time. He really didn't have a choice.

AN HOUR LATER, HE HEARD THE FRONT DOOR SLAM. "HONEY, I'M home."

"I'm in the kitchen," he called. With the help of another pill he'd managed to make a chicken pasta and salad for their dinner. "All Kendra's fashion needs sorted, then?"

She came to him and wrapped her arms around his neck and kissed him. Dinner was forgotten, as his need for her swamped him. She broke off the kiss to put the ice-cream in the freezer.

"Did you rest?"

"I'm not eighty."

"I know," she said. "But your back's been sore today, hasn't it? I hate seeing you in this much pain."

"Actually, Sully came by." He looked at her face and sighed. "You knew."

"I—we—just thought you needed someone other than family to talk to." She stood there biting her bottom lip, hope and anxiety in her eyes.

He should be angry, but it made him see that Stella really did love and care for him. Did she love him? Did he love her? He didn't want to lose her. "You'll be pleased to know I've made an appointment with Dr. Forrester for Thursday to talk about the operation." He'd talk to her about the rest of it after the ball. He wanted her to decide whether she was in or out. He wanted her to hear everything before she committed her life to him.

She squealed with joy. "I'm coming with you."

That was the idea, because Dr. Forrester wouldn't hold back. She would finally understand why he'd been so reluctant. "Thank you. I'd like having you there by my side."

She moved back into his arms. "I'll always be by your side as long as you want me."

He wanted her, all right. The pill he'd popped was working its magic. "How hungry are you? We could always heat it up later?"

"The only thing I'm hungry for is you."

Marcus put a lid on the chicken pasta pan, and turnied off the heat. Their mouths remained locked in a tangle of tongues and their hands began undressing each other as they walked or shuffled toward the bedroom.

When they reached the bedroom, she quickly shimmied out of her skirt and lacy black underwear.

Marcus reached for her. She was wet and wanting. She made him lie on the bed and slowly crawled over him so she could finish undoing the buttons on his jeans. She pulled them down his legs loving that he was commando. His erection sprang free, and before she could do anything, he reached in his sideboard for a condom and tore it open, rolling it down over his hard length. "Come on, Stella. I want that slow ride you promised."

"Are you sure, Marcus? I don't want you to stuff your back. I want you on my arm tomorrow night—"

"Get that sweet ass over here. I don't give a goddamn about my back right now," he added. "Another part of me is aching and only your sexy body can ease the pain."

Taking him at his word, she climbed onto his lap and straddled him. His gaze never left hers as he guided her slowly down, gradually filling her. Her head fell back on a long sigh as heavenly sensations surged through her.

His large hands skimmed over her hips and up her sides until he cupped her breasts. He teased her nipples with his thumbs and heat pooled where they were joined. Looking down at him, she covered his hands and urged him to squeeze her breasts harder. She always loved his hands on her body. Marcus kneaded her firm flesh making her crave more.

Marcus loved that Stella showed him what she liked. Even after he'd had her every which way but Sunday, he still needed more. He couldn't remember the last time he'd wanted someone so intensely. He'd always want her. He pulled her down towards him so his mouth could reach her delights. Her beautiful breasts and rosy pink nipples drew his hands and mouth. Playing with them and teasing her with his tongue made him throb.

The more he sucked on her nipples, the more restlessly she moved her hips until she braced her hands on his shoulders and rose and fell. She had a body built for sex, and he wouldn't let his pain interfere with enjoying everything she offered.

Her smooth, lightly tanned skin was a little flushed, and her toned arms and thighs did all the work. The desire in her eyes mesmerized him, heightening his own passion.

After the shower earlier today, Marcus concentrated on her needs. He would make it last as long as possible for her. "You're so fucking beautiful, Stella. I want you to come for me again and again. I love how responsive you are."

She smiled at him as her breath quickened. "I don't want to wait either. You turn me on with that bad boy smile. You're sexy and I love it. I love having you inside me."

He smiled in acknowledgment before capturing her mouth in a searing kiss. Her lips were so soft and lush, and he remembered her expertise in giving head. Grasping her hips, he urged her into a faster tempo while trying to conserve his back, but he couldn't help the odd thrust upwards.

She clutched his shoulders as she moaned, and he felt her tight heat clench around his rigid shaft. Sliding his hand between their bodies, down her stomach to her mound, he stroked her, providing double titillation. His reward was hearing her scream as she collapsed onto his chest and trembled in his arms.

Her pulsing muscles pushed him over the edge and he couldn't hold back anymore. He let a powerful release rock through him, chasing away the pain. His Stella. *Never leave me.* Marcus pressed his face into her neck as he groaned in pure ecstasy. It held him for a moment before fading away.

"We are so going to do that again tonight, sweetheart."

She slid down to lie on top of him. "Promises, but I want you to be honest about your pain. I've never been into pain and pleasure. I'd hate to find out I'm hurting you."

"Don't worry about me. I'll let you know if it gets too bad."

"I really want you with me tomorrow night. Do you realize it will be the first time we have been out in public as a couple? I want to show you off."

He stroked the satiny skin of her buttocks. "I won't let you down for tomorrow night."

"You better not or I might just have to threaten to go with Jason Colter."

She was teasing him, but a small niggle of doubt hit him. He was damaged and other men were not. Would she eventually grow tired of his disability?

Fuck. He'd said it, even if only to himself. He had a disability. His back was fucked beyond all recognition, and he needed to deal with it. Sully was right, he was being a pussy.

He started tickling Stella. "I'll tickle you to death until you retract that terrible threat."

She squealed and wriggled in his arms. "I take it back." He kept tickling. "I'll go with Carey Stevenson then."

"When will you learn? You're mine." He found her mouth and turned her squeals into moans.

CHAPTER EIGHTEEN

S tella closed the front door of the apartment on her departing glam team. Leigh had done her make-up and Jackie her hair. She wrapped the dressing gown around herself as she walked back towards Marcus's room—their room. All she had left to do was slip on her dress and Jimmy Choo strappy heals. Leigh had helped her put on her jewelry, and she loved the weight around her neck. She rarely wore jewelry, but she loved the glamor once in a while.

Her stomach clenched, tied up in knots that she bet even an experienced sailor couldn't undo. She hated public speaking, but tonight in front of two-thousand guests she had to speak. It was her charity, and her guests, sponsors and staff deserved her thanks. It was funny that having Marcus there gave her courage. She wished she could give him the same courage.

Her heart was still all gooey and warm that he was seeing Dr. Forrester next week, about the operation, and most of all, letting her come with him. At last he was letting her in. Their relationship had turned a corner.

She entered the bedroom to find Marcus sitting on the end of the bed, fully dressed, except for his jacket. In his white dress shirt and pale blue tie to match her dress, he looked like a movie star and her breath hitched. "God, you're handsome as sin. I'll be the envy of every woman there."

"Until every woman learns, I can't put on my own Goddamn shoes."

That's when she noticed the shoe overturned on the floor and the one in his hand.

"Let me help you. You can play Cinderella and I'm the Prince looking for my true love." She got down on the floor and picked up the shoe and grabbed a sock off the bed. It was a black patent Oxford Men's dress shoe that laced up the front. The polished shine was almost blinding.

"I should have bought the slip-on dress shoes instead of the one's that tie, but I wasn't an invalid back then."

She glanced up as him as she lifted his foot. "You're not an invalid."

"Look at me. I can't even bend down to put my bloody shoes and socks on." He threw the other shoe in his hand across the room. It crashed against the tallboy sending the vase on top crashing to the floor. Water and flowers went everywhere.

She took a deep breath and, looking at the floor, counted to ten. This was the first time Marcus had ever thrown a pity party, and she thought his true feelings were better out than in. She ignored the damage and continued to put the shoe she held in her hand onto his foot.

She stood up. "I'll just get a mop."

"Don't do that. Don't treat me like a child."

"Then stop behaving like one."

"You don't know what I live with every—"

—"You're right. I don't, but that's because you won't let me in. I can't imagine the pain and fear you face every day, but I want to. I want to help. To comfort you. To be someone you can lean on—rely on."

"I don't need a babysitter." The words spit out in bitterness.

She shook her head and sighed. She simply collected the thrown shoe, put on a sock and placed it on his foot, which seemed to make the situation worse. She could almost see the steam coming out of Marcus's ears. She would not cry.

She crossed the room and picked up the damaged flowers and walked out to get a mop. Luckily, the vase hadn't broken.

When she walked back into the bedroom with the mop, Marcus still sat on the end of the bed, forlorn and looking like a lost little boy. Her heart melted.

He looked at her. "I'm sorry. It's just so frustrating to have to rely on someone else. I'm not used to being helpless."

"At some point in our lives, we all have to rely on someone else, and when you love someone, you want to be there to help them. Don't push me away because of pride."

"I'm going to be the biggest prick to live with for a while."

She walked over and hugged him. "As long as the biggest prick loves me and wants me with him, I'll take it." She pressed a kiss to his hair. "Besides, big pricks give the greatest pleasure."

He laughed, and just like that the mood lightened, and the night was looking up again.

She cleaned up the mess and then went to the guest room to slip on her dress.

Once she was happy with the way she looked, she made her way to the living room. Marcus waited there for her, and he let out a long whistle as she entered and her confidence soared.

"Jeez, I'll be fighting off the other men with a stick. Perhaps I should rethink not taking a walking stick."

She'd suggested Marcus use a walking stick around the house while his back was bad, but she couldn't quite get him to agree. That pride thing, or was it fear that once he did, he would be on the slippery downward slope to a cripple. "You look so beautiful."

"Right back at ya' big guy. I think I'll be borrowing that stick to fight off the ladies. The limo is waiting downstairs. Are you ready to go?"

"Almost." Marcus pulled her to him and kissed her. "Thank you for being with me. I'll try not to be a grouchy old bear. I love you."

Tears welled. "I love you too."

"Let's go raise a ton of money for your charity."

"I'm sure we will. The event sold out so quickly and we have some amazing auction items."

When he turned to collect her wrap, she noticed his face grimace. He'd been so good at taking only the prescribed meds. It would be a long night. "Give me a moment. I just need to touch up my lipstick because of your kiss." With that, she hurried to their room and the ensuite. She grabbed his bottle of OxyContin from the drawer and stuffed it into her clutch bag. She didn't want him to be embarrassed, or made to look helpless tonight. She wanted to keep his pride intact for now. Perhaps, just for tonight, he could have more pills to help him through the night.

THEY'D ARRIVED EARLY AND STELLA HAD LEFT HIM WITH TOM AT the bar while she worked with the team to ensure the programme would run like clockwork.

"She really is Wonder Woman. I suspect the night is much harder to organize then she and her team make it look."

He nodded in agreement at Tom's words.

Kendra added, "She is such an amazing woman. Most women with her looks and money simply live the life of leisure, but not Stella. I should try to do more."

Marcus smiled. "You have more commitments; children and your music. You do what you can." He remembered how loyal Stella had been when Kendra was diagnosed with cancer in her early teens. She stayed by her side, held her hand when they shaved off Kendra's hair, shaving her head at the same time, and defended her against the silly children who made fun of her. Stella would never leave him if the worst happened. He didn't know if that was a good thing or a bad.

He looked across to where she was surrounded by people. She laughed at something Carey Stevenson said, and it became glaringly obvious to him he was one lucky son of a bitch to win the heart of Stella Perry.

"Are you going to bid on any item?" Tom asked as he flicked through the programme.

He hadn't really decided. He didn't want for anything but a strong and pain free back. "Don't know. You?"

"There's an amazing luxury family holiday to Kenya, visiting the safari parks. It might be worth doing before all the animals are no longer freely roaming the planes."

"Isn't Matti a bit young for that?" Marcus asked.

"Yeah. Maybe I'll go for the trip to New Zealand. Lexie has been raving to Kendra about it."

"We could all go." He looked at Tom. "But I might be out of action for a few months."

Tom smiled and slapped him on the shoulder. "Thank fuck. You're going to have the operation?"

"I think so. I can't go on like this. This week Stella wanted to get me a walking stick."

"Kendra will be pleased. She hates knowing you're in such pain. We'll all be here to support you as you recover. Don't worry about Bad Boy Autos. Miami will have to wait."

"About Miami..."

Tom spoke before he'd said more. "I don't really care if it never happens. I love my life as it is. I don't need more than a fantastic job, great friends, and my loving family."

"Good. I'm not saying never, but I have enough on my plate for now."

A waiter walked past with a tray of champagne. Marcus shook his head and turned to the barman and asked for a Coke. He'd taken his evening allowance of pills, but he'd also brought extra with him. He couldn't drink at all tonight because it wouldn't mix well with the additional OxyContin, and he'd do nothing to ruin Stella's night after all her hard work.

The scent of her perfume in the air told him she'd joined them. He turned, smiling. "Everything okay."

She slipped her arm through his. "The MC will get everyone seated for dinner shortly. I won't be able to relax until I've welcomed the guests. How's your back holding up?"

"Fine. Don't worry about me, and concentrate on making this a wonderful evening for all and raising loads of money."

Just then, Catherine and Carey joined them. Catherine smiled, saying, "This is going to be such fun. There are so many people here and already I've already heard them fighting over which auction lot they want to win. I feel money is in the air."

"That's good. It's such a great cause. Can you imagine going through life struggling to read and write?"

"Shall we take our seats? We're right in the middle at the front." Stella led the way. All the Bad Boy Autos team was seated on this table. Tom and Kendra. Catherine and Carey. Lexie and Kade. Sully and one of his women. They hadn't been introduced yet. And of course, he and Stella. He was looking forward to a good meal and the company.

As they made their way through the crowds, all sitting so the event could begin, they passed Jason Colter with a beautiful blonde on his arm. "Black, how's the back?" Jason thought he was so funny. Marcus wished he could punch the guy in the face, but Jason was driving for his company so he simply pretended he'd not heard.

"Sometimes I wonder what Lexie ever saw in him. Kade is so different from his brother. Jason is so obnoxious," Stella said under her breath.

"Even he won't get to me tonight because I have the most beautiful woman on my arm and it's your night."

Once they were seated, Stella reached for her champagne and took a long swig. At Marcus's raised eyebrow, she said, "What? I'm nervous. I hate public speaking."

"Yet you do it so well," Kendra said.

"I have to. Raising money is all about visibility. There are so many in need and not enough money to go round."

Marcus squeezed her knee under the table. "When you're up there, just look at me, sweetheart. And once you introduce the evening, you can relax and we can enjoy a night out."

She cupped his cheek. "What would I do without you?"

Before he could reply, the MC announced her, and she made her way like a bejeweled butterfly to the stage.

Her speech was so heartfelt, and the room grew eerily silent as she spoke. She spoke about what the literacy charity was trying to achieve, the results they'd had so far and what they wanted from this event. The statistics of 1 in 6 children dropping out of school unable to read and write was shocking, and he saw the looks on everyone's faces. She issued them all a challenge. To imagine they couldn't read the menu on the table or the items listed up for auction. How would that change their evening?

By the time she finished thanking her staff, sponsors and those attending, she got a standing ovation.

He'd never been so proud.

When she arrived back at the table, he kissed her in front of everyone and she hugged him as if she never wanted to let him go.

They held the auction in-between courses. They'd just finished the first course when Marcus glanced at the catalogue and an item caught his eye. A beautiful diamond and sapphire ring from one of the most prestigious jewelers in LA was in the auction. As soon as he saw the picture, he knew it would look beautiful on Stella's finger. Was he really thinking of proposing? It was as if someone had walked over his soul. He turned to look at her and just knew. He loved her. Really fuckin' loved her.

He excused himself and moved through the room until he found Damian Shelburne, the Porsche dealer who had donated a car for tonight's auction, and his friend.

"Marcus, great to see you. Your girlfriend has really turned on a super night."

"She and her team have, and it's thanks to the generosity of people like you that we'll raise a shitload of money for a graeat cause. Speaking of which, I have a favor to ask."

With that, he explained what he wanted his friend to do.

"No limit?" Damian asked.

"No limit. I want that ring."

Damian looked across the room to where Stella sat looking like a princess in her pale blue gown. "She looks worth it."

"She is and so much more."

This would be a wonderful surprise for Stella and whatever it cost, the money was going to her charity. They shook hands, and he returned to his seat via the restroom. Even though Stella had organized cushions for his chair, sitting for extended periods killed his back. One more pill would help, so he popped one.

As he made his way back to the table, the auction for the ring was underway and there was fierce bidding. "Tom put your hand down. I don't need another ring. I'd prefer the trip to New Zealand."

"But the ring is gorgeous," Stella said. "I might bid for it myself."

Shit. "Perhaps you could bid on an item that's not so popular?" Marcus suggested.

She looked crestfallen. "I guess so. I'd hate for any donor to feel like I didn't appreciate their item. But that ring is beautiful," she repeated.

Lexie leaned in and whispered in his ear, "Bid on the damn ring, she wants it."

"Who says I'm not," he replied with a wink.

"I'm liking you more and more," she whispered.

"I have my moments."

"What are you two whispering about?" Stella asked.

"I was grilling her about the vintage Jaguar she drove in NZ. I wanted to know if it was for sale."

"Is it?"

"She doesn't know, but I have the owner's contact details. I might look into it." He picked up Stella's hand and kissed her knuckles. "Maybe once I've had the operation and I'm recuperated, we could see it together."

"Way to go, man. You're having the operation?" Kade interrupted. "No one told me."

"I haven't really told anyone, except Stella."

"When? When's the op?" Sully asked.

"I'm discussing it with Dr. Forrester this week, but I'd prefer it sooner rather than later now that I've decided." He didn't want to have time to think about all the things that could go wrong. Just in case he changed his mind.

"That's fantastic news. Let's have lunch at my place tomorrow. The entire gang. We haven't done that since before Lexie and Kade's wedding," Sully offered.

"Not too early. I'll need a sleep in," Stella laughed. "But I'd love to. Thanks, Sully."

There was so much talking around the table that Marcus almost missed the hammer falling on the ring at three-hundred and seventy-five thousand dollars. When he looked across the room, Damian gave him the thumbs up.

He didn't know if it was because the pill he'd popped had kicked in, but he'd never felt so high. Now he just had to think of the perfect time to give it to her.

While Tom took Stella to the dance floor, he made his way to Damian's table.

"You owe me four hundred thousand dollars."

"I thought it was three hundred and seventy-five." But Marcus smiled. "I'll organize the money first thing on Monday. I'll collect it from you then."

"Stay and have a drink. I'd like to introduce you to Andrew Gardner. He needs a car conversion, and I thought your team might manage it."

He could hardly turn Damian down when his friend had forked out all that money on the ring on his behalf.

He beckoned to a man sitting on the other side of the table. "Andrew, come meet Marcus Black. He owns Bad Boy Autos and he could help with the Aston Martin you just won."

Andrew looked about mid-thirties. Marcus waited for Andrew to stand, but it took him a few minutes to realize Andrew was in a wheelchair.

Andrew pushed back in his wheelchair back and came around the table to talk with them. Marcus stuck out his hand.

"It's your car, isn't it? I saw your name on the programme. You donated it."

"Very true."

"So you'd definitely be the best to make a few alterations for me so I can drive it."

"I have to admit we haven't done that kind of work before."

"I'm willing to take a risk if you are. I don't want the car's unique selling points to be altered if you get my drift. I might be stuck in this chair, but I want the car to fly. I've heard they're chick magnets."

"Perhaps you should come into the shop one day next week with the car and talk with the team." Marcus wanted to ask how he'd ended up in the chair, but knew it wasn't polite. All he could see was the chair and how everyone around Andrew looked at him differently. Treated him differently. Hell, he was. Normally he'd say straight away that it wasn't the work Bad Boy Autos took on, but he didn't want to say that to a man in a wheelchair.

"I'll ring and make a time. Nice to meet you," he said and he wheeled himself off.

"He's a mixed-up guy," Damian said. "Broke his back coming off a horse playing polo. The first operation was a success, in that he could walk, but gradually his back pain got worse. They'd told him he'd eventually end up in a chair, but he'd hoped to put it off for longer. He's had several operations until the last one, which didn't work."

The words, *this could be you,* resounded repeatedly in his head and he could feel the sweat running down his back.

Marcus's mouth dried. It was as if he was looking at his own future. The woman sitting with Gardner didn't seem to be very attentive. Damian noted what he was looking at.

"His wife left him last year. Can't say I blame her. He didn't take his change in circumstances well. He must've been hell to live with. That's his escort and I mean that in every sense of the word."

He looked toward the dance floor and saw Stella dancing with Tom, enjoying herself. She danced as if she didn't have a care in the world. He looked at the woman sitting next to Gardner. She looked bored and resentful. She too looked at the dance floor, but with longing.

A wave of nausea hit, and he needed to get some fresh air. He hurried towards the terrace and burst out into the night, gulping for air, his body shaking. He saw a server and called him over, grabbing a glass of champagne from his tray and downing it in one while reaching for another.

He moved to stand at the rail. It was a warm night, so he took his jacket off and flung it over the back of a chair. He stood there, letting the alcohol flood his already drugged system until he felt nothing.

How stupid was he? How on earth could he expect a woman like Stella to live with half a man?

A pinwheel of images whirled in his brain, a brain befuddled by booze and pills. He tried to think straight. He stared out at the city below. Sully was right. He was a pussy. He'd needed her to help make this decision that would irrevocably change his life. He'd wanted her there to hold his hand. He knew she wouldn't leave. He'd been selfish, but he couldn't do this to her. Not to a woman as lovely and full of life as Stella.

He breathed in deep, trying to get the oxygen hit that might chase away the smothering fog, but it didn't. He took another swig of champagne, but that only made it worse.

A hellish ache compressed his chest.

He didn't know what to do.

He swore into the night as frustration rose, and a blinding, bitter anger descended. How the hell was he supposed to let her go when he knew deep inside his life would be miserable without her? But hers would be miserable with him. Letting her go was the best thing to do, for her. For the woman he loved.

He might be a selfish asshole, but seeing Andrew Gardner tonight was like a lightning bolt to the gut.

For once in his life, he would be unselfish, and let her go.

CHAPTER NINETEEN

Stella couldn't believe how much money they were raising. The amount surpassed her wildest dreams, but that wasn't why she was so happy. It was having Marcus by her side. Her boyfriend. Her lover. Her best friend.

She'd danced with quite a few men this evening, feeling free and happy. Marcus couldn't, or maybe the best word is, shouldn't dance, but he'd promised to slow dance when Kendra sang her ballad. She looked around in time to see Marcus leave Damian's table and head out onto the terrace.

She rose to join him via the restroom.

"You look happy," Catherine said as they made their way to the ladies.

"I'm very happy."

"Because of the auction or the man?" Catherine chuckled. "Or both?"

"Both."

Catherine sighed. "It gives me hope. If a player like Marcus can settle down, then maybe Carey can too."

"So, it's Carey you've fallen for."

"Yes, but he treats me like his kid sister. He's my older broth-

er's best friend. He only asked me to be his date tonight, so he
didn't have a woman on his arm who would get ideas. Let me
tell you, I have plenty of ideas and they involve both of us
getting very naked—together."

"I suggest some slow dancing up close. That ought to get him
going". It was Stella's turn to laugh. "With you in that dress it
would get a priest going."

"I live in hope."

"Speaking of slow dancing with a hot hunk, if you'll excuse
me, I need to find Marcus. I saw him slip out onto the terrace.
He promised me a dance to Kendra's song, and she's up next."

The smile on her face was so wide she hoped she'd fit
through the doors.

The first thing she saw when she stepped outside was
Marcus with his jacket off, leaning against the balustrade. The
second thing she saw was he had a glass of champagne in his
hand. The third thing was his arm around Holly Carpenter, a
recent ex.

The smile on her face dimmed.

She could see from how he was standing and the goofy
look on his face that he was high and drunk. Perfect, bloody
perfect.

"Here she is, Saint Stella. Ssh, don't tell her I'm drunk."

Even Holly looked embarrassed, as she slipped out of
Marcus's hold. "Nice to catch up, Marcus. Call me some time,"
she said, and slipped away like a bad smell.

Stella didn't want to have an argument here. Not on her
special night, and not with a man so high he could almost touch
the moon.

She noticed his jacket hanging over a chair and collected it.
As she laid it over her arm, a pill bottle fell out. She bent and
slowly retrieved it from the tiles. She turned it over in her hand
and read the label. OxyContin. A strong dose too, prescribed by
Dr. Andy from Maui.

All this time. He'd been hiding this from her all this time.
What else had he been hiding?

He must think her stupid; checking his pills every day,
ensuring he was following the doctor's orders when all along
he'd another supply hidden away. She rattled the bottle in his
face, anger growing like an extra limb. "Care to explain?"

He shrugged and almost fell over. She caught him before he
could do more damage to himself.

"You've been lying to me."

"Not exactly. You asked me how many pills I'd taken from
Dr. Forrester's prescription." His next mistake was to smile as if
that was so clever.

She wondered why steam wasn't coming out of her ears, but
now was not the time to lose it. Plenty of time for that when
they got home. She slung his jacket over her arm and reached
for his elbow. "I'm taking you home. You're in no condition to
go back inside."

He shrugged out of her hold. "You should stay. Enjoy your
night. I'll find my own way home."

"We came together, we go home together." *Where I'll tear a
strip off you for lying.*

"It's not your home, it's mine."

She took a step back, stunned. Something was going on here.
Something other than taking too many pills. What had
happened during the night? Who had he talked to? It couldn't be
about Holly, could it? Did he suddenly realize what commitment meant?

No. This wasn't about another woman. She knew Marcus's
faults and dumping her at an event for another woman wasn't
in his make-up. He was arrogant and proud, but never
purposely mean. That's one of the reasons she loved him. He
came across as a gruff, arrogant playboy, but underneath he was
a marshmallow.

"Why are you acting like this? What's happened?"

"I've had a change of heart about a steady relationship. It's been brought to my attention that it's not what I really want."

She drew in a deep breath. Was it about Holly? Something hard glittered in his eyes—cutting her heart with diamond-tipped blades. This was not the Marcus she knew. Even drunk and high, he'd never talked to her like this before, or looked so menacing.

"I'm not talking to you in this state. I'm taking you home and I'll go back to my apartment for the night if that's what you want, but we are not doing this here. On my night." She could barely hold back the tears. This was supposed to be their night. The first official function as a couple and he'd ruined it.

Just then, Tom and Jason appeared. "Hey, Kendra's about to sing. I thought you wanted to dance."

Don't say it. Don't' say it. But Jason had to open his mouth. "High as a kite, Black. You called me all the foul names under the sun when I was an addict. Looks like the shoe's on the other foot, dope head."

"Fuck off, Colter," Marcus slurred, and took a drunken swing at Jason. The swing went wide and Marcus fell into Tom's arms.

She looked at Tom with watery eyes. "He's high and drunk. He's in no condition to dance. He needs to go home."

"My home," he said and beat his chest. "Can Stella stay at yours tonight? I don't want her at my place when she's all angry."

Her pride hit the floor, and Tom's mouth firmed into a grim line.

Colter butted in again. "Hey, Black. Stella's welcome to stay at mine anytime she wants."

Instead of telling him to fuck off, Marcus simply shrugged. "It's up to her."

His careless disregard for her broke the dam inside, and the pent-up hurt and anger burst from her. "Care to dance?" she asked, and she grabbed Jason's arm and led him inside to the dance floor, her emotions tossing around inside her like a ship in a storm.

"He's an addict. Don't take it personally. Tonight he doesn't know what he's doing."

She wanted to believe Jason, but Marcus wouldn't drink on top of the drugs unless he wanted to cause a scene. He knew what it had done at the wedding. "You're wrong. He drank on purpose."

Jason pulled her into his arms as Kendra sang her beautiful ballad. "All not well in paradise?"

She laughed. "Obviously not. I just don't get it though. He's agreed to meet with Dr. Forrester to schedule the operation. Everything was fine until tonight. Something has happened."

"I saw him talking to Andrew Gardner earlier at Damian's table. Was it anything to do with that?"

"Who's Andrew Gardner?"

"He's the guy in the wheelchair who broke his back a few years ago playing polo. After several operations, he was left in a wheelchair. Most of the time he's a miserable bastard. He's never gotten over his disability. He's letting it eat away at him."

"That's unkind. It must be a huge adjustment to go from fit and healthy and walking around, to being in a wheelchair." Hence why Marcus got loaded tonight. She wanted to smack her forehead. She had to put herself in his shoes. How would she feel if faced with her worst nightmare?

"Crap." Jason said. "Marcus's operation." He looked sad. "Man, he's going to need some help, and I don't mean physical. He needs therapy to face what might be coming. I feel like an asshole for goading him."

"And I just walked off and left him hurting to dance with you." She wished she could go back and simply take him home.

"Stop chewing that bottom lip. Let him sleep it off. He'll be a different man in the morning. I always was. Until I got high again."

But Jason was right. She alone couldn't help Marcus through his fear. It was time to bring in the experts. She'd ring Dr. Forrester in the morning.

∾

"WHAT THE FUCK IS WRONG WITH YOU? THIS WAS SUPPOSED TO BE Stella's magical night. How could you? If you weren't my best friend and Kendra's brother, I'd give you a bloody good thrashing. But then I shouldn't hit a man who's drunk—and high."

"She won't leave me."

"What are you fucking talking about? Why would she leave you?"

"You're not listening. She won't leave me. I just know it." He tried to take a step but fell sideways, Tom's quick hands catching him. "She has to leave me. What if I end up in a wheelchair like Gardner?"

"Who's Gardner?"

"The guy in the wheelchair at Damian's table."

Tom's mouth formed an O. "Now is not the time to feel sorry for yourself."

"It's not me I'm pitying. It's Stella. The woman with Andrew is miserable. How can I risk chaining Stella to a man who can't give her the life she deserves?" He wobbled, so Tom propped him up with his arm around him.

"Shit. Where's Kendra when I need her? Right. She's on stage. I'm missing my wife singing for this shit." He grabbed Marcus's jacket. "I'm going to pour you into a cab. I'm not missing the rest of the night because you're drunk. It's the first night out in months for Kendra and I. Dad's babysitting and we're staying at the Beverley Hills Hotel."

Marcus didn't care. He was beyond feeling anything. He would give Stella up.

Inside he was already dead.

As they wound their way through the crowd inside, towards the exit, Tom saw Lexie and Kade and beckoned them over. "Any chance you could take Marcus home? He's in a bit of a state."

"Mixing pills with booze never works," Lexie said. "We'll take him home. We'll stay with him until Stella gets home."

"You might be there all night. She's pretty mad. I'm not sure if she'll there tonight."

"He's got a spare room. I did this many times for my brother, Jason, when he was an addict." Kade slipped his shoulder under Marcus's shoulder. "You go to your wife. We've got him."

The last thing Marcus remembered was pain as he hit his head on the cab as Lexie pushed him none too gently into the vehicle.

CHAPTER TWENTY

Stella arrived back at Marcus's at around eleven the next morning. She'd slept at her apartment. She'd wanted to phone Dr. Forrester and have a clear head before she faced Marcus. As she'd thought, this was a common coping mechanism for those facing an unknown future. The surgeon was already arranging a therapist for Marcus. All she had to do was get him to agree that he needed help.

She'd messaged Lexie last night and told her of the plan. They'd agreed to stay until morning to ensure Marcus safe. They were just leaving as she arrived.

"He's all yours, and he comes complete with a head like a pissed off bear, so be warned."

"Thanks, Lexie." She kissed her friend on the cheek. "Wish me luck."

Lexie hesitated before she closed the door. "He loves you, I know it. The first thing he asked about this morning was you. Were you okay?"

"But does he love me enough?"

Lexie nodded. "One word of advice. Love shouldn't be too hard."

Stella laughed. "Define too hard?"

"For me it was being hurt over and over again. Apologies get weary after a while. I think you've given him plenty of opportunities. The man needs to grow up and deal with his life. If he can't do that with you, then he needs to do it without you. For your sake." She hugged Stella. "It's hard to admit defeat and let go, though. I'll be here if you need me."

Stella leaned against the closed door and let the silence in the apartment descend. Was Lexie right? Would Marcus deal better without her? Was she enabling this behavior? Was he taking these pills and delaying the operation for her?

She went to the kitchen and made coffee for them both and took it down to their—his—room. She couldn't knock because she had her hands full, so she pushed the door wide and entered.

He was lying on his back, half covered with a sheet, but naked from the waist up. He didn't even turn his head to look at her. Was he ashamed? Or was he so hung over any movement of his head sent pain roaring through? She hoped it was the latter.

She put his coffee on the nightstand by the bed. "I thought you might need this." He didn't move. "We need to talk. We can do it now or I can come back later."

"I don't want to talk."

God, he sounded like a sullen little boy. "I don't really care what you want. I think you owe me an explanation and an apology regarding your behavior last night." She sat on the end of his bed as he sat up, and she handed him the coffee. "I think I know what set you off, but I want you to tell me. Let me in. Let me understand what you're feeling."

Marcus remained silent for a few moments. "I don't think it's a good idea to start a relationship when my entire world is about to change."

"Start? This started long ago. Our relationship hasn't just started. What's just started is the commitment you made to me to try for something more. I think you're using the surgery as an excuse to push me away because you're scared of commitment. Scared of being only with me."

He looked at her then. "I might end up in a wheelchair."

"You mean like Andrew Gardner? So? I'm aware of that."

He looked away. "Why would you want to stay with me, then? Relationships are hard enough when everyone involved is fit and healthy."

"Oh, my god. Is this what your freak out is about? Not the fact you might end up crippled, but because I might leave you? My parents marry more often than bunnies breed, and your parents can't bear being in the same room. Some marriages fail —get over it. Most don't fail. Yet you've decided you shouldn't commit because marriages don't work and I'll leave you because you're in a wheelchair."

He just sighed. "You don't understand. I might end up like Gardner, nd he's not taking it well. I'm pretty bloody sure I won't either."

"That's a bloody excuse, and you know it. You're using Gardner and what 'may' happen after your op as a means to push me away because it frightens you to lose. You're frightened of losing me. You're scared this is all getting too real and you might fuck it up. Well, good job. You're fucking it up now."

His face paled. She didn't let up, hoping he'd man up. "I get it. Love is scary. You're vulnerable. You can get hurt. Be made a fool of. Lose everything. But it's also wonderful, sharing a life, children and family. There's no better joy. Isn't the reward worth the risk?"

Would he admit it? "Not to me." He ran a hand through his hair and she willed him to say more, to talk to her.

When he didn't, she got angry. "Why can't you trust me? Trust in the fact I love you. Love isn't only for the good times. What's the vow, in sickness and in heath?"

He looked determinedly at her. "We should have left our relationship as friends with benefits, where no one gets hurt."

She stood up with her hands on her hips. "You mean you won't get hurt. Me, I'd take the risk any day. I took a risk you'd love me enough to get over your fear of marriage."

He just stared at her, his jaw clamped shut.

"I guess you've got what you wanted. I want a relationship with a man who loves me enough to trust me. A man who will share the journey together, the good and the bad. I want a man who will fight to make our love work. You're giving up at the first hurdle, albeit a pretty big one. If you don't have faith in me to be there when things go wrong, then I can't be there when they're right. You either trust in my love or not. I'm not willing to risk you leaving every time life gets tough."

He didn't correct her or ask her to stay. He just sat there like a marble statue. Unfeeling. Uncaring that she was about to walk away.

She stood and walked to the door. "You know what cuts me up inside, is that you stood by Kendra. You never left her side, yet you have so little faith in my love to do the same for you. I don't think you know me at all. Perhaps sex *was* all we shared."

MARCUS HEARD THE DOOR SLAM BEHIND STELLA AS SHE LEFT. Grief swamped him, but he knew he'd done the right thing letting her go. She deserved a man who loved her, a man who could give her all the things in life she wanted. A good life with children and a home and stability.

He lied down again and closed his eyes. He'd done the right thing, hadn't he? Now he could concentrate on getting his back better without having to worry about how the outcome might affect Stella.

He rubbed his chest, which for once was hurting more than

his back. The room was silent, and he missed her already. Her scent lingered, taunting him as he tried to fight the self-pity engulfing him.

He tried to remember when they'd only been friends with benefits and realized he preferred what they shared now. He liked being that close to someone, letting her into his life. But he hadn't let her in. He'd pushed her away like the coward she'd accused him of being.

He had to live with that decision.

CHAPTER TWENTY-ONE

O n Thursday morning, Marcus visited the bank on his way to his appointment with Dr. Forrester. The beautiful sapphire and diamond ring he'd bought at the auction went into his safe deposit box. It was pointless keeping a ring of that value in his home. There would be no woman he'd ever want to give that to. It was, and always would be, Stella's ring.

He missed her. She constantly filled his thoughts. Especially today of all days. Stella gave him the courage to make this appointment.

Marcus sat in the waiting room of Dr. Forrester's office.

His palms were clammy and his heart beat built towards a small gallop. He was here to start the long journey of his back operation. The receptionist, Mandy, was surprised he was here alone. She'd told him to ring someone as it was a lot to take in and it helped to have someone here taking notes to help him, and he would have someone to talk over the information with.

The only person he longed to have by his side, he couldn't. *Stella*. He missed his Stella.

He'd phoned Kendra. She was on her way.

The lift doors pinged open and a man about Marcus's age exited using a walker. He shuffled in and smiled an acknowledgement to Marcus, before turning to the receptionist.

"Hi Mandy. I'm a bit early."

"That's okay, John. There's one patient in before you."

"You, I take it?" John addressed Marcus, extending his hand.

"Marcus Black," he replied, as he shook it.

"John Gallagher. My wife's parking the car. Usually she still beats me here even with having to park the car." As he spoke, the lifts opened again, and a woman stepped out. A very pretty woman. "There's Anna now."

His wife sat down beside him. "You beat me today. It's not often I lose."

John nudged her. "I'm like a speeding turtle at the moment. I won and you know what that means later tonight."

She blushed prettily. "Not here," she whispered.

They looked happy together and Marcus couldn't help but grin at the undercurrent of what John would win tonight. He suddenly realized he didn't think of John as disabled when watching them together. "Do you mind me asking what you're here for?"

John looked him over. "First visit, huh?" He looked at his wife. "I broke my back in a car accident. I was hit by a drunk driver. The car flipped, and I was trapped in the wreckage. I'm here for another operation to see if I can get more mobility. You?"

"Car wreck too. No drunk driver, or maybe it was."

John leaned forward. "I know that name. Marcus Black. You were in Formula One until the accident."

He smiled. "Yes, that accident. The back pain is a bitch and I can't live on pain meds forever, worse luck."

John nodded. "I highly recommend getting rid of the pain."

"As do I," Anna said. "He was like a bear with a sore paw, and as grumpy as shit."

"I don't know how she put up with me."

"I love you, you idiot." The look they shared tore at Marcus's heart. This was the kind of love stories were written about. He could see it in the way they looked at each other. The way they touched. He thought of the elderly couple on the boardwalk by the beach in Maui he'd watched at Lexie and Kade's wedding. They'd had it too. It made him realize love like that did exist.

He could have had that with Stella.

Did she love him enough to survive what might be thrown at him? He'd not given her a chance to prove she could, because he'd decided for her. Was it because he doubted his love for her? Would he want her with him if he was healthy and not facing this nightmare?

Hell, yes, he wanted to scream. It was because he was afraid. Afraid she'd leave him, so he'd pushed her away first.

"I hope you don't think this is too personal, but did your accident affect your marriage in any way?"

"God, yes," Anna said. "You must know how it is. You're a fit man in your prime and then you can't walk properly, or do the things you used to do, and the pain is constant. I was the metaphorical punching bag who copped all the anger."

"Did you ever think about leaving him?"

She nodded, while John added, "I'm so very lucky she loves me so much."

"I understood his pain, but it was my pain too. I'd lost the man I had married. I could have left or stayed. I stayed. I loved him so much I wasn't willing to throw that away. I suggested counselling, and we worked through the change in our life." She sat silently for a moment before adding, "I can't say there aren't things I miss, like dancing, and every trip has to be planned because of the problems with walking long distances, but then I think about what my life would be without him, and I'm just thankful that drunk driver didn't kill him, because even with him like this, he's in my life and my life is wonderful."

"Are you married?" John asked.

"No, but I have—had a girlfriend."

"'If she left you, she wasn't the one," Anna said confidently.

"She didn't leave me."

John laughed. "You pushed her away, huh? Yeah, been there. I tried to do that when I learned I might not walk again."

"It's hard to walk away when you're married and I loved him," Anna said.

Stella didn't fight very hard to stay. She hadn't been in contact with him since the day after the ball. Perhaps she didn't love him enough. That's what he was afraid of. If they were together and then she left... Pushing her away hurt like a wound from a snake bite right now, but if she left him later, because he wasn't whole anymore, it would hurt more than he could endure.

"If you love her, then let her in." John's words were spoken quietly. "How can she love you if you don't share what's going on in your head? They're not mind readers. Counseling taught me that."

Before he could ask more, the lift opened again and Kendra hurried out.

"Sister? She looks so much like you." Anna smiled.

He was just about to introduce her when Dr. Forrester walked out, and they had to go. Before he walked away, he turned to John and said, "Thank you. Both of you. I have some thinking to do."

John handed him a business card. "Pleasure. Good luck, and if you ever need to talk, call me. I know I wished I'd had someone to talk things through with."

Marcus looked down and saw that John was an attorney. Like Marcus, at least he hadn't lost his livelihood. He had a job he could still do. "I'll do that."

～

HIS MIND SPUN WHEN HE CAME OUT OF THE MEETING WITH DR. Forrester. Kendra was wonderful. Apparently, she and Stella had already talked a lot of this through with Dr. Forrester, hypothetically, of course.

He'd underestimated her. Stella had known what she was getting into, and she'd still stayed.

He couldn't stop himself. He needed to know. "How's Stella?"

"How do you think? Heartbroken, but trying to put on a brave face. She's not taken a minute to rest since the ball. She's got straight on with ideas on how to raise money for your new charity. She's even had a meeting with Father, and you know how she hates dear old Dad for what he did to me. Apparently, she read him the riot act and then some."

He stood by his car in the parking garage. "I've really fucked up."

"You'll get no argument from me. What's this all about? Stella says you don't love her enough. That you don't trust her. Is that true?"

He sighed. "I love her so much. I thought setting her free of all of this was the thing to do. If I'd met John and Anna at the ball instead of Gardner, maybe I'd have done things differently."

"Why did you tell her to go then?"

"I didn't want her to be stuck with a cripple, and she was right, I didn't trust her. I was sacred she'd leave me when things got really bad and I don't think I could have coped with that."

Kendra moved in to hug him. "See her. Tell her what you've told me. Let her hear what you're thinking and feeling."

"What if it's too late?"

"Stella has a very forgiving heart. She's forgiven father. She loves you, and if you truly love her, you'll come through this operation and what life throws at you with bells on. You know Tom took a risk in loving me, with deciding to build a life with me. We don't know what life holds for us, if my cancer comes back…" She swallowed hard. "But even if it does, I've had the most wonderful love and I have my children. Loving someone is worth the risk when they love you back. Love is all powerful. It gives us the strength to go on and endure. It makes us happy. It's never something to be afraid of. Grab it while you can."

Marcus hugged her tight. "Thanks, sis. Love ya'."

"She's at home today. She got a little rescue puppy yesterday, and she's playing mummy. The dog was going to be a surprise for you to help take your mind off everything and to keep you company while you recuperate."

"Any suggestions on how I go about this?"

"Lots of groveling. And flowers." She got in the car. "Come for dinner tonight. I'll make enough for two because I have faith in my brother, and in the fact that Stella loves you."

She got into her car, and Marcus waited for her to drive away.

For the first time, Marcus understood what he'd given up by pushing Stella away. He wanted a team-mate, not a support person. He wanted Stella on his team, fighting alongside him to beat this injury. He ached for her strength and loyalty and—please, God—her love.

He turned to the Dodge. He had one stop to make before he visited Stella.

CHAPTER TWENTY-TWO

S tella sat in her garden courtyard under the shade of the umbrella. Kendra had just called her to tell her how the appointment went. Stella wished she didn't care so much, but how did you just suddenly stop loving someone?

She'd thrown herself into her charities. It hadn't worked.

She hated that Marcus had to go through his back operation without her. She knew he was strong, formidable even, so she wouldn't bother pushing the point home, that she loved him enough, and she didn't care if he could walk or have a family with her, as long as she had him in her life.

He had to come to that realization on his own because she couldn't take him distancing himself when things didn't go as planned.

But what if he didn't? What if he thinks because you didn't fight for him, you don't love him enough?

Just then she heard a little yap, and she looked down to see Bailey had woken up and was chewing her sandal. "Hey, little minx. No chewing," and she pushed her away. "Go toilies." Bailey was a clever little ten-week-old Cavoodle. She trotted off and did her business and came running back for the treat she knew she'd get for doing the right thing.

Stella scooped the chocolate-colored puppy into her arms, and they sat in the shade together. "At least you know how to love me." As soon as she said the words, she smiled and could have hit herself.

That's probably why Marcus was so bad at love. When they'd tried for a real relationship, he'd told her he'd never been in love before, that he'd probably make mistakes and to bear with him. He didn't know how to do this.

She shouldn't have simply walked away. She'd sent him the wrong message.

He needed her to fight for him. He needed to know that she loved him so much nothing would ever destroy that—not even a wheelchair. She needed him to know he was her world and always would be. She'd called him a coward, but she was being one too.

She should be brave and risk everything by not giving up.

She bent down and picked up Bailey. "Come on, my little girl. We're going to surprise Marcus."

AS MARCUS PULLED INTO HIS PARKING GARAGE, DISAPPOINTMENT weighed heavily on him. Stella hadn't been home. He'd rung Kendra, but she didn't know where Stella was.

His imagination had gone into overdrive. Who was she with? Was she seeing someone else already—Jason Colter?

He opened the front door and almost stepped into a little puddle of water. WTF?

A tiny bundle of fur hurtled towards him, but slid to a stop at his feet, looked up, took in the size of him, and turned tail and ran back towards the living room, yapping as if the big bad wolf was after it.

But Marcus's world brightened instantly because he knew who that puppy belonged to.

He walked into the living room, and there she was. Standing by the window, the little puppy hiding behind her legs, growling.

"I'm sorry, but I still have a key so I let myself in."

"It's great to see you. I was at your house. I need to talk to you."

"I needed to talk to you too."

He hoped she wasn't here only to give him his key back, but having the puppy with her was a good sign, and his heart felt lighter than it had in days. "Shall we sit down, and we can talk to each other," he offered. "But first, who's this?" and he bent as much as he could and cooed at the puppy, ignoring the pain as his back spasmed.

"Bailey. She's a Cavoodle."

"And very cute." Bailey came forward and sniffed him curisouly, allowing herself to be petter. Like every other female, Marcus had her eating out of his hand. He scooped her up, standing slowly and suggested they sit on the sofa.

"I've made a mess of things."

She nodded. "You told me you would. You've never done love before."

"It's been an adjustment."

"And you have enough adjustments what with your back situation and the surgery," Stella sighed.

He wanted to deny her words, but he couldn't. Although she sounded so wistful it gave him hope.

"I used to be that guy. That guy who had everything in his life he wanted. Money, a great job and tons of attention. Like any hot-blooded male sex was on top of my list, but never commitment. Like you, my view of marriage was distorted. Then, one night in a bar, you got in my face and I knew you were different. Different because I wanted to see you again, but because I didn't want to look too closely at why, and because the idea of a relationship scared me to death, and I'd be in Europe and you'd be here, I gave what we shared the name of friends with benefits."

She smiled. "I talked about looking for Mr. Right, but when I met you, you became my Mr. Temptation. I'd always wanted you, but given I was friends with Kendra, and you had a well-deserved wicked reputation, I thought it a bad idea. That night in the bar, I thought, what the hell. I had to have you and I didn't care if it was only for one night, until the next morning. When you left, you took a piece of my heart with you." She shook her head and laughed. "When you suggested friends with benefits, I fooled myself into thinking that was all I wanted. Until Tom came back into Kendra's life and I learned there was so much more I wanted. With you. Only you."

"I can't be Mr. Right." It hurt him to say it. "Mr. Right sounds too perfect, and I think if you expect Mr. Right I'm always going to let you down. I'd much prefer to always be your Mr. Temptation."

Her face fell. "Hot sex. Is that all you want? Do you want to go back to FWB?"

"Oh, honey, I want much more than passionate sex from you. I want your laughter. I want your strength. When you slip that tiny hand in mine, everything feels right with the world. I want your kindness. Your intelligence. Your need to make the world a better place for everyone. I need you by my side for the rest of my life, but most of all, I need your love." He gave a stuttered laugh. "Besides, if this operation goes sideways, I'm not sure I'll ever be up for sex. That's why I pushed you away."

Her mouth formed an O. "Dr. Forrester explained there were ways"—

—"Don't let me focus on that. I just didn't want you to be saddled with that kind of life. You deserve so much more. Be honest, you love sex and you want children. While it might not be impossible with me, it sure as hell won't be easy or fulfilling."

"Isn't that my choice?"

"Absolutely, but you were right when you called me a coward. Worse still, I couldn't bear making you miserable like my parent's relationship. I'm a risk taker, we all know that, but I calculated the risk was too great. It scared me to love you. Petrified me that you might leave, because I know I won't go quietly into a wheelchair. It's not my nature and I might take it out on you. But then I realized I could bear a wheelchair, but I couldn't bear losing you. "

"I'm a risk taker, too. Did you know that about me? I have to be, because I risked my happiness on a man who'd never loved before. A player. A man who took a long, long time to face that we'd been in a relationship since that night in the bar. I took a risk that you could love me enough. Do you? Do you trust in my love? Because if we are to face what is coming, trust in each other is vital. I don't want to drive down this road with you if you'll crash and burn at the first bend. I don't want my heart crushed either."

He pulled her until she was sitting on his lap. "The visit this morning to Dr. Forrester revealed that you and my sister had visited him. He told me you two got down into the nitty gritty of my condition. It made me realize if you started this race with me, you were in it to win it."

"I love you. I've loved you for a very long time and it feels wonderful to admit it."

He brushed back her hair, his gaze unwavering and true and his smile sure. "I love you too. And I feel so humbled to have won your heart. It's the greatest victory I've ever had or ever will."

"I hope not. I hope the greatest victory is you being healthy and pain free."

"If I have you, it doesn't matter as much if I'm not."

She pressed her lips to his and he was lost himself in the kiss until her bottom disturbed the hard little box hidden in his pocket. He broke the kiss and pushed her off his lap. He stood and pulled out the box from his pocket. She gasped.

"Shit. I haven't thought this through. If I try to go down on one knee, I might not get back up."

She stood tall on the sofa. Bailey thought it was a game and began yapping. "Now I'm taller than you and it looks like you're on your knee."

He lifted the lid and tried to ignore the little puppy. "Stella Perry, my beautiful girl, will you make me the happiest man in the world by becoming my wife?"

"Oh, my goodness, Marcus, that's the ring from the charity auction."

"I wanted to propose that night, until I had a freak out." He waited, holding his breath. "I understand if you want to wait until after the operation."

She jumped off the couch and threw her arms around his neck. "Yes. Yes, I will marry you. I'd marry you tomorrow, but Kendra will kill me if I don't have a big fancy wedding."

"We could always drive to Vegas tonight, get married, and still have the big fancy wedding once I can walk you, pain free, back down that aisle as my wife."

A huge smile broke on her lips, and he wanted to kiss her so badly. "I love that plan, but what about Bailey?"

He looked down at the little puppy sitting at his feet, tail wagging, picking up on their excitement. "She's part of our family so she gets to come too."

As if Bailey understood, she started yapping and tried to crawl up Marcus's legs.

"Seems like another female has fallen in love with you."

"There's only one woman I want in love with me and she's in my arms. Forever."

CHAPTER TWENTY-THREE

They'd got through Thanksgiving even though Marcus was full of pain meds, but now, just before Christmas it was time for his surgery. A pain free Christmas was unlikely as he'd still be recovering, but he wanted to start the New Year with a new chance at a pain free life.

Marcus thought he'd be nervous, but he really just wanted this over with. He was ready to face whatever was to come, with Stella firmly by his side.

He'd checked into the hospital this morning.

All the Bad Boy Autos team had squeezed in, probably against the rules, but in this private hospital, they didn't seem to mind. The noise in his room relaxed him. Everyone was talking at the same time.

It was two months since he and Stella had eloped and got married in a small chapel in Vegas. Kendra forgave them, only because the she and Stella were already planning the main event for next summer, after his operation and recovery. Speaking of which, he looked across the room to where Stella sat with Bailey on her lap.

Stella filled his heart with so much joy, but damn, he also

loved that little dog. This morning, Bailey saw them packing a suitcase for his hospital stay and there was no way they were leaving her behind. It would be good for Stella to have something else to concentrate on during his surgery.

He loved the calm smile she threw his way. Soon they would come for him. The operation would fuse his spine and hopefully take away the pain. They were also checking the steel rod that was in his upper back. The doctors thought it might be pushing on a nerve causing more pain.

Dr. Forrester would assist only. He'd obtained the services of the best orthopedic surgeon in the world. A surgeon from England, Mr. Bann. Marcus thought about those in the world who couldn't afford what he could, and another charity idea formed. He'd talk to Stella after the surgery.

A nurse arrived in the doorway. "If you'll excuse me, everyone, it's time. Clear the room, please. Only Stella can stay."

"Good luck, man." Sully shook his hand.

"Thanks for agreeing to fly to New Zealand to check out that Jaguar for me."

"No problem. I need a change of scene. You know how much I hate Christmas." Sully lost his kids sixteen years ago on Christmas day when he was still drinking and his wife got custody. He was a different man now. Bad Boy Autos would be lost without him. "I'll see you when I get back."

Catherine kissed his forehead. "You've got this boss."

"Absolutely."

"I'll keep them in line while you 're away."

"I bet you will. Thanks, Catherine."

Lexie had her arm linked with Kade's. They both smiled at him. "Catch you on the other side."

Then came Kendra and Tom. Kendra was crying. "It's going to be fine, sis. I have the best surgeon in the world."

"I know, but I just want it to work so badly for you both."

"We'll wait with Stella." Tom was choked with emotion, too.

"Thanks for being there for both of us."

"Always."

And then the room was empty, and it was only Stella and Bailey. She came to sit on the side of his bed as the nurses bustled around them. He had a horrible shower cap thing put on his head and his pre-meds given to him.

They were taking effect as his eyelids were drooping.

"Stella," he whispered, "Stella, I love you."

"I love you, too," she replied and she bent and kissed his lips, almost squashing Bailey in the process. "I'll be here holding your hand when you wake. The same as I will be every day from now on."

"We're a team."

She followed his gurney from his room all the way to the operating theatre, and only then did she let go of his hand. Bailey cried in her arms as they took him away through the doors, and the last thing he said was, "I'll be back," like the terminator and the last thing he heard was Stella's laughter.

EPILOGUE

Two years later...

The sound of a crying baby invaded Marcus's sleep, and then an elbow thrust into his rib, followed by a sleepy, "Your turn."

Marcus pushed back the covers and padded to the cot on the far side of the bedroom. Tiredness weighed down every step, but as soon as he looked at his five-month-old son, Dean Thomas Black, his world brightened. He bent and picked his son up without a stab of pain.

Life was good.

Bailey wagging her tail as she followed them into the kitchen, where he heated a bottle of Stella's breast milk.

Two years on from his operation, his life was much more than he'd ever expected. It was so damn close to perfect he sometimes wondered how he'd got so lucky.

He'd had a long recovery time, as the damage was more than anyone expected. The rod between his shoulders, had moved out of place and they couldn't believe he'd survived in that much pain for so long. He should have shared how bad it had gotten earlier. His fitness and muscle mass helped him immensely.

His worst fears over the operation never eventuated. He could walk, he might not be able to run a marathon, and his days of driving small sports cars were over, but he wasn't a cripple in any sense of the word.

Months of physiotherapy and swimming saw him recover faster than anyone had thought. He'd gone back to work four months after his operation. He'd put Miami on hold because his heart was in Los Angeles with Stella. This was their home.

He sat on the sofa in the living room, baby Dean snuggled in his arms, drinking his milk as if they never fed him. Marcus turned on the TV and played their wedding clip they'd watched this afternoon with his parents, talking to his son the whole time.

"This was you mother before you were born or conceived. Isn't she beautiful?"

Little Bailey raced up to the TV barking as she watched Marcus walking down the aisle with Stella on his arm, Bailey behind them. It had been the happiest day of his life—until little Dean was born.

"What's all this noise?"

Stella plopped down next to him and stroked Dean's head.

"You should be sleeping. I've got this."

"My two favorite men are out here. Besides, I love this clip."

"That's funny, it's my favorite too."

"Yeah, I love looking at Mr. Right."

"You mean Mr. Temptation," and he wiggled his eyebrows.

Stella stifled a yawn. "Nope. When I'm tired and you're feeding Dean, you're definitely Mr. Right. Mr. Temptation will have to wait until I've had more sleep."

"Sweetheart, I'd wait for you forever."

He turned to look at her, but she'd already fallen back asleep, cuddled against his shoulder.

He looked down, and he saw Dean was snoozing, too.

He smiled.

Stella was right. To have this love. This deep, all-consuming love was worth any risk, because the reward was utter contentment.

She was also right about something else. When you get love right—when you meet your Mrs. Right, or Mr. Right, don't ever let them go.

He wrapped his arms around his family, his heart swelling with happiness.

He'd go through all the pain again without complaint, knowing he'd have this.

Love.

Because love is all you need.

WANT MORE BAD BOY AUTOS?

Fast Track To Love For Christmas 99c Novella

Want to see more of Sully? I've a novella of Sully finding his perfect someone in the

BABY IT'S HOT OUTSIDE : A CHRISTMAS DOWN UNDER BOXED SET

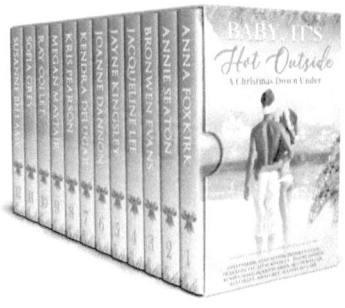

It's only 99c on pre-order releasing 25 October 2021 then the price will rise to $4.99.

Here's a snippet:

Fast Track To Love This Christmas
   By Bronwen Evans

Bronwen set this Christmas romance in her home town of Havelock North, a hero for her heroine, but he's a visitor from the USA... Bron hopes a hero like Sully comes calling...

Kara turned and dangled the keys to the Jaguar in her fingers. "She's in good working order, but she's, as you say, vintage. But then you're a mechanic should she get temperamental."

"I can handle temperamental," and he moved closer.

"I'm sure you can."

Sully moved closer again. "This lunch tomorrow. Shall I pick you up in the Jag? If so what time? And is it casual?"

She swallowed back the desire to run her hand down the muscled chest that was only inches from her. "It's at a winery, outdoors, so it will be hot. A hat and smart casual will do. It's in aid of a charity that raises money for a primary school lunch programme for the lower decile schools in Hawke's Bay."

"That sounds like a good cause. Is primary school little kids? Elementary school we call it in the States. I didn't know NZ had such poverty."

"Most countries do, don't they? Primary school is from five until about ten years of age. How can we expect kids to sit and learn when they're starving. And if they don't learn we can't defeat the poverty cycle."

He reached out and ran a finger down her cheek. "It sounds like you're quite passionate about this. It's a fabulous cause. Anything that can help kids rise out of poverty gets my vote."

She shivered at his touch. This man was turning her insides out with just a smile. *Slow down, girl. Don't go getting real feelings for this man. He's not a keeper.* "I'm on the charity board." She didn't mention the charity was her baby. She'd built it up from nothing with a group of deep pocketed and time rich like-minded people. "Yeah, I am completely passionate about this. Loads of kids didn't have the fortunate upbringing I had, and I want to help even the score." Her ex had said she was wasting her time. She would prove him wrong.

"The world needs more people like you." The warmth in his eyes made her bottom lip tremble. "What time shall I pick you up outside the hotel? Or do you live elsewhere?"

"I live on the top floor of the hotel, the opposite end to your suite. So let's say 11.30am as I need to be there by 12pm and it's about a twenty-minute drive."

She really should move away from the car but her feet wouldn't step away from him. Finally, she said keeping her voice light, "Have a good day. Remember to drive on the left," and she skipped round him and headed back to the elevator. Once again she could feel his eyes following her every step.

For one fleeting moment she wished Sully wasn't stirring her senses so much. He was the first man in a long time who affected her this much. She was beginning to hate the fact he would be leaving, returning to America, and that was dangerous.

Why did she always fall for the wrong men?

Fall? Nope. No way. Never.

Fun was what she wanted.

Only fun.

BUY LINK:

ABOUT BRON

USA Today bestselling author, Bronwen Evans grew up loving books. She writes both historical and contemporary sexy romances for the modern woman who likes intelligent, spirited heroines, and compassionate alpha heroes. Evans is a three-time winner of the RomCon Readers' Crown and has been nominated for an *RT* Reviewers' Choice Award. She lives in Hawkes Bay, New Zealand with her dogs Brandy and Duke.

Thank you so much for coming along on this journey. Reviews are always welcome and help authors immensely. So does talking with your friends about what you enjoyed in the book.

If you'd like to keep up with my other releases, my newsletter coupon codes for specials, or other news, feel free to **join my newsletter** and receive a **FREE** book too. You can also join the newsletter on my website.

www.bronwenevans.com

ALSO BY BRONWEN EVANS

Historical Romances

Wicked Wagers

To Dare the Duke of Dangerfield – book #1

To Wager the Marquis of Wolverstone – book #2

To Challenge the Earl of Cravenswood - book #3

Wicked Wagers, The Complete Trilogy Boxed Set

The Disgraced Lords

A Kiss of Lies – Jan 2014

A Promise of More – April 2014

A Touch of Passion – April 2015

A Whisper of Desire – Dec 2015

A Taste of Seduction – August 2016

A Night of Forever – October 2016

A Love To Remember – August 2017

A Dream Of Redemption – February 2018

Invitation To Series

Invitation to Ruin

(Winner of RomCon Best Historical 2012, RT Best First Historical 2012 Nominee)

Invitation to Scandal

(TRR Best Historical Nominee 2012)

Invitation to Passion

July 2014

(Winner of RomCon Best Historical 2015)

Invitation To Pleasure

Novella July 2020

Imperfect Lords Series

Addicted to the Duke – March 2018

Drawn To the Marquess – September 2018

Attracted To The Earl – February 2019

Contemporaries

The Reluctant Wife

(Winner of RomCon Best Short Contemporary 2014)

Coopers Creek

Love Me – book #1

Heal Me – Book #2

Want Me – book #3

Need Me – book #4

Drive Me Wild

Reckless Curves

Purr For Me

Slow Ride

Fast Track To Love At Christmas - novella

Other Books

Baby It's Hot Outside: A Christmas Down Under Box Set

A Midsummer Night's Romance Boxed Set

Dukes By The Dozen Anthology Boxed Set

Christmas In Kilts Anthology Boxed Set

Winter Wishes: A Regency Holiday Boxed Set

Highland Wishes And Dream